A GENTLEMAN'S INTEREST

Bridget looked down at her leather breeches and scuffed boots. She dressed like a man and worked like a man. But she could never *be* a man. She could never control her own life and make her own choices. Thank God Papa understood her. Another father might have forced her to marry—or even to accept one of the lords who'd come sniffing around, talking about establishments of her own. As if she'd consent to be kept! As if she cared about jewels or fine clothes. She had her horses. That's all she wanted, all she needed.

Her gaze found its way to Lord Haverly. He was a good-looking man—tall and dark, with a hawkish nose and eyes of deep black. Strange how she felt when he'd put his hand on her shoulder—a kind of excitement. Something like the exhilaration she felt when she was galloping Waterloo—and yet different.

Lord Haverly wasn't a horse. He couldn't be trusted like a horse could be trusted.

She leaned her head against the stallion's fragrant warm side. "I'm being silly about this," she whispered. "His Lordship's come to look at the horses. That's what's got his interest. That's what we sell, after all. Horses— nothing more."

His Lordship's Filly

Nina Porter

ZEBRA BOOKS
KENSINGTON PUBLISHING CORP.

ZEBRA BOOKS are published by

Kensington Publishing Corp.
475 Park Avenue South
New York, NY 10016

Zebra and the Z logo Reg. U.S. Pat & TM Off.

First Printing: December, 1993

Printed in the United States of America

for another Bridget

Chapter One

Andrew, Marquess of Haverly, watched the lad lean forward, pushing the stallion to his limits. As the great chestnut lengthened his stride, eating up the track, Andrew whistled softly and turned to the portly man beside him. "He's a goer, all right. You've got yourself a fine one there."

"Aye." Grinning, Victor Durabian pushed his tweed cap to the back of grizzled red hair. "He loves to run, that Waterloo does."

Andrew smiled, glancing around. He'd spent several years fighting Napoleon, and several more on his return to England in getting the estate at Haverly back in shape. When he left, Tattersall's had been the place to go for horses. But while he was gone, Durabian had moved his business down from Ireland to a farm outside the city. Durabian's stables were small, but his paddocks were well-kept and it was easy to see his horses were prime stock—the best around Peter said—and worth going the extra distance to see. And now that he'd been here, Andrew could easily believe it.

"Raise him yourself?" he asked.

"Aye. From a spindly little colt." Durabian chuckled. "He's a fierce 'un, can't bear to be beat."

"I can understand that." Andrew turned back, watching in admiration as the rider finished the course, slowed, and guided the magnificent animal toward them. The horse had superb lines and the handsomest head he'd ever seen.

The boy on his back was a fine rider, too, and, if the red hair peeking out from beneath his cap was any sign, probably one of Durabian's progeny.

His cap pulled low, the boy brought the horse to a halt in front of them and swung lightly down. "Great ride, lad!" Andrew said, clapping him heartily on the shoulder.

The boy turned, whipped off his cap, and glared at him with the iciest green eyes he'd ever encountered. Female eyes! With a sense of shock, Andrew took in the tangle of fiery red hair that had tumbled loose. This was no boy. This was a woman, a full grown, beautiful woman.

"Ye've no call to cut his Lordship to pieces with yer eyes, girl," Durabian said briskly. "If ye will go about in that male getup, how's he to know?"

The green eyes didn't lower their hard gaze—if anything, they got even icier. And the girl didn't move, just stood there, glaring at him.

"Me daughter Bridget," Durabian said cheerfully. "This here's Lord Haverly, Bridget. Friend of Lord Peter, he is."

The girl vouchsafed Andrew a brief unfriendly nod.

Her father smiled at him. "She loves the horses, Bridget does. And Waterloo here, he's her pet."

He coughed apologetically, blushing under his daughter's burning gaze. "To tell the truth, milord, it's Bridget what raised the stallion. She what had the training of him."

Andrew extended a hand to the girl. "Please accept my apology, Mistress Durabian. And my congratulations. You did an excellent job. I've never seen a finer animal."

"Your apology is accepted," she said crisply, her cultured tones contrasting oddly with her father's broad Irish brogue. But to Andrew's dismay, she completely ignored his outstretched hand. "As long as you keep your hands to yourself, we'll have no trouble."

What a shame! The looks this girl had—and the tongue of a shrew. "Very well," he conceded. "Then we should deal famously together. *And* my congratulations?" he went on, his curiosity piqued in spite of himself by this aggravating creature who carried herself like a queen, a queen in shabby leather breeches and scuffed boots. And a white shirt that, now that he was really looking, didn't hide the swell of an intriguing bosom.

"The horse is a wonder of himself," she said, conceding nothing and meeting his most engaging smile with a look of cold disdain. "He needed very little training." She turned and led the animal away, an arm thrown familiarly round his neck.

"Don't mind her," Durabian said, pulling out a well-worn pipe and a pouch of tobacco. "She's apt to be a bit on the tetchy side, Bridget is."

Andrew nodded, regretfully averting his eyes from the tantalizing sway of leather-clad hips. "Isn't it a bit unusual—I mean—" He ground to a halt. Liking Durabian as he did, he was reluctant to offend him.

But the Irishman merely chuckled and tamped his pipe.

"If you're meaning why do I let me daughter go round in men's clothes and mess about with horses like a lad—I'll give ye a simple answer. Truth is, milord, I can't hardly stop her. Headstrong, Bridget is. Real headstrong, like her mama."

Of course, this tantalizing creature had a mother. How could the woman—Andrew turned. "Her mother lets her—?"

"Her mama's gone," Durabian said, crossing himself with a sigh. "She died birthing Bridget. She were a lady through and through, though her family would have none of her after she run off with the likes of me. We were that happy." He swallowed. "But I lost her. And so I had the raising of Bridget meself." He sighed again and lit the pipe. "I hadn't the heart to give her out to a wet nurse to raise, so I kept her by me. Prob'ly it were wrong, her being a girl and all. And no woman about the place to teach her the right of things. But—"

"I think I understand," Andrew said. "And who's to say what she should learn. She's—" He hesitated again.

"She knows horses better'n any man." Durabian chuckled. He turned and looked Andrew straight in the eye. "And she's a looker, milord. Ye needn't quail at saying it. I've had plenty others say so."

Andrew frowned. He could see Durabian's quandary. A daughter like that could well draw buyers, but if she was rude to them—and she certainly knew how to be rude—Durabian's business could suffer. It was obvious the man had loved his wife. And just as obvious that he loved his daughter. So this couldn't be an easy thing for him.

"I'm surprised some lord hasn't made off with her,"

Andrew said. "Or that some honest fellow's not offered marriage."

Durabian puffed heavily on his pipe. "Honest fellows *have* offered," he replied, "but she'd have none of 'em. And as for lords—" He shook his head. "They've tried, too, lots of 'em, but Bridget ain't got no use for quality. On account of how bad they treated her mama afore she was born."

"I guess that's understandable," Andrew said. "Loyalty's an admirable characteristic."

"Thank 'ee, milord. Bridget is that—loyal no end. She do worry me, though, her being me only child and her not wanting to marry. I never married agin, ye see. Mayhap that was a mistake, too. But I loved her mama something fierce." He sighed again. " 'Tis sad, my Bridget not being a lad, but—"

"Sad?" Andrew clamped his mouth shut before he could finish his thought. The girl's father wasn't likely to appreciate his saying that such a gorgeous creature shouldn't be relegated to a stable.

"So, 'twas Lord Varley that sent ye here," Durabian went on, changing the subject.

"Yes," Andrew said. "He told me you had some great horses." He smiled ruefully. "He didn't tell me about Bridget, though. If he had, I'd have been more careful."

Durabian nodded. "His Lordship treats her like another lad. 'Tis the best way, milord. She'll be civil to ye then." He chuckled ruefully. "At least I hope so."

"I'll hope so, too," Andrew said. He looked toward the stable where the girl had led the horse and was preparing to unsaddle him. "That stallion's one marvelous animal. How much do you—"

"Saints preserve me!" Durabian whispered, his ruddy face growing even redder. "I should have told ye, milord. Don't be after wanting *that* stallion. 'Twill do ye no good, ye see."

Andrew raised an eyebrow. "You mean he's not for sale? You must have had some good offers—a great beast like that."

Durabian shook his grizzled red head. "Not that I wouldn't like to sell him. Or at least to see the blunt I'd get for him. But I daren't even think of it, milord. He's her heart, that stallion. Her heart and her soul." He puffed at his pipe. "If I separated 'em, milord, well, I'm afraid the girl would up and die on me. She's that attached to him, she is."

Andrew gazed out across the paddock. He loved horses, too. It wasn't that difficult to imagine her attachment to that magnificent creature. To lose such an animal . . .

He himself knew loss. The pain, the struggle just to go on living. When he'd come home from Spain to find his brother Thomas dead, struck down by disease, he'd thought his own life had ended. As in a sense it had. Thomas had been the oldest son—the heir. With him dead, the mantle of inheritance had fallen on Andrew's shoulders. And it was a mantle he didn't want—had never wanted.

Before Napoleon's delusion that he could conquer England, Andrew had enjoyed the life of the man about town: horses, prize fights, the theater, and an occasional bit of fluff. A good life—quite satisfying. But now everything was different. *He* was the Marquess of Haverly. He had a duty to fulfill, a name to live up to. He had Thomas's place to fill.

"I hear tell ye bought a nice-looking filly from Tattersall's of late," Durabian said. "What'd ye call her?"

"I call her Sable," Andrew said. "She's a real beauty. Rather on the touchy side, but she can run. Still, I don't know that she could rival Waterloo."

Durabian chuckled. "So that's her name—Sable. I've heard, though, that she goes by another."

"Oh." Andrew raised an eyebrow. "And what other is that?"

"They call her 'his Lordship's filly,' " Durabian replied, his eyes twinkling with suppressed merriment.

Andrew was not surprised. "Do they indeed?"

"Aye. And they say ye had a mite of trouble taming her. But ye did it and she's fast, very fast." He looked a little dubious. "They say she might even be able to take my Waterloo. Not that *I* believe such a thing."

"I don't think I care to race her," Andrew said.

"Ye don't?" Durabian didn't sound surprised. "And why is that, milord?"

"A friend of mine recently fell into bad times because he was too fond of wagering on the horses. And I don't think I want to put others in the way of temptation."

Durabian's ruddy face broke into a scowl. "Wagering can bring a man low, all right. That's God's own truth. I ain't always been the carefulest about such things meself." He looked around. " 'Tis Lord Peter Varley ye're talking 'bout now. I heerd he come a bad way. Wichersham, wasn't it, who had his vowels?"

Andrew nodded. "But fortunately Peter's friends were

able to pay his IOUs and keep him from being sent to debtor's prison."

Durabian knocked his pipe against a post, emptying it. "Wichersham's the worst sort. I seen his cattle. His stock ain't healthy. Ye can tell a man's character from the look of his horse, ye know. And that man's horse shows he ain't friend to no man, nor animal neither."

He gave Andrew a sideways glance. "Most of us in the business knows which of Lord Varley's friends it was what bought up his IOUs. Ye're a good man, milord."

Andrew sighed. Could nothing be kept secret in this town? "I didn't want that known. I'll thank you not to spread the story about."

"As ye wish, milord." Durabian put the pipe back in his pocket. "Shall we be taking a look at the stock I do have for sale?"

Outside the stalls, Bridget frowned, stuffing her hair up under her cap again. That lord had startled her, clapping her on the shoulder like that.

Most of the men who came here knew better than to touch her. And if they didn't, they soon learned. Why couldn't this one just mind own business? Why did he have to come round in his elegant clothes, lusting after the horses she loved? If she could, she'd have kept all the horses they raised. Each one was like a child to her, a piece of herself. But Papa was right—he did have to make a living. And to do that he had to sell horses.

But he wouldn't sell Waterloo, not ever Waterloo. Waterloo was hers. Papa had promised.

She ran a hand down the stallion's warm flank, relishing the feel of taut muscle and smooth coat. "You're such a beauty," she crooned. "Such a marvelous beauty. And you're mine, all mine."

She threw the saddle and blanket over a bench and reached for the currycomb and brush. "You like this," she told him. "I know. It feels good."

The horse whiffled, thrusting his nose at her playfully. "No more sugar," she said, stroking the velvet spot between his nostrils. "Too much sugar will make you fat."

That lord—that Haverly—wasn't fat. She risked a glance at him over the horse's back. He wasn't fat at all. Lean and fit, he looked quite elegant in his fine clothes. But clothes didn't make the man. Under his finery this man could be just as bad as the others—always trying to get her alone, always trying to put his hands where he shouldn't, always wanting what a woman shouldn't give a man—unless he was her husband.

But maybe this Lord Haverly was like his friend Peter. She liked Peter. He treated her like another man. Like an equal.

She glanced down at her leather breeches and scuffed boots. She dressed like a man and worked like a man. But she could never *be* a man. She could never control her own life and make her own choices. Thank God Papa understood her. Another father might have forced her to marry—or even to accept one of the lords who'd come sniffing around, talking about establishments of her own. As if she'd consent to be kept! As if she cared about jewels or fine clothes. She had her horses. That's all she wanted, all she needed.

She looked Haverly's way again. He *was* a good-looking man—tall and dark, with a hawkish nose and eyes of sparkling black. Strange how when he'd clapped her on the shoulder that odd feeling had run through her—a kind of excitement almost. Something like she felt when she was galloping Waterloo, exulting in the raw power between her tight-gripped knees, something like that— and yet different.

But Lord Haverly wasn't a horse. He couldn't be trusted like a horse could be trusted. He was a man—with all a man's wants and failings.

She leaned her head against the stallion's fragrant warm side. "I'm being silly about this," she whispered. "His Lordship's come to look at the horses. That's what we sell, after all. Horses—nothing more."

Chapter Two

"Well," Andrew said later that evening when Peter joined him at a table at White's. "You were quite right. Durabian has some really prime stock." He sent his friend a knowing look. "You might have warned me, though."

Peter dropped into his chair with a grin. "You mean warned you about Bridget?"

Andrew snorted. "Of course I mean Bridget. Why didn't you tell me about her?"

Peter chuckled, his eyes mischievous. "I take it your famous smile didn't melt her."

Andrew grimaced. "Melt her? Indeed not. Nothing would melt that ice maiden."

"Oh, I don't know." Peter reached for his glass of wine. "I've seen her with the horses. She's another person then, warm and loving."

Andrew straightened in suspicious disbelief. "Good Lord, Peter, you're not—"

Peter shot him a sharp look. "No, I'm not in love with her. As you know, if and when I marry, it'll have to be to money. And I'd never seduce Bridget." He grinned again.

"Even if I could. Now you, you're the one who brings beautiful maidens to their knees. Always have."

"Don't be asinine." The idea of Bridget on her knees to a man was ridiculous. Besides, since he'd taken over Thomas's duties as marquess—or more accurately had them pressed on him—his previous behavior did seem frivolous. "With looks like that she's far more likely to seduce *me.*"

Now what had made him say such a stupid thing? He was the head of his family. He had no time for dalliances with stable maids. And he was certainly not the sort to take a maiden's innocence. He limited his female forays to the lightskirts whose business it was to serve male needs—and who had no innocence left to lose.

"So," Peter said, picking up his wine glass, "did you acquire some new horseflesh today?"

"Not yet. But I thank you for the tip about Durabian's place. There's a bay colt there I have my eye on."

Peter nodded, his eyes twinkling. "Just so it isn't a particular filly."

Andrew caught his meaning immediately. "I doubt any man will ever tame Bridget. So I guess I'll follow your lead and treat her like a man."

"Yes." Peter sighed deeply. "But that would be so much easier, wouldn't it, if she didn't insist on wearing those leather breeches!"

Frowning, Victor Durabian watched Bridget put the stallion through his paces. The girl was getting too pretty for her own good. He was worried about her future—a girl like that alone in the world. He wasn't going to live forever. If only he could find a good solid husband for her.

He shook his head. Even if he could, Bridget wouldn't be having any husband.

He turned away. He had other problems to occupy his thoughts. Too bad Haverly hadn't found a horse he wanted to buy. A hundred pounds would come in mighty handy about now. He kept his creditors more or less paid up, but there was the matter of his racing IOUs. As he'd told his Lordship, he knew the dangers of wagering on the horses. But he just couldn't seem to stop. And he'd been losing too much, too often, lately. The blacklegs, the bookies, were all right. They wouldn't take his bet anymore without the money up front. It was the other wagers that were bad, the ones he'd made on the side, the ones he'd given IOUs for.

The holders of his notes had not yet put him in prison for the simple reason that once there he couldn't raise any money. But they wouldn't be patient forever. He had to do something, and do it soon.

Too bad he couldn't sell Waterloo. Haverly would buy the stallion in a shot. But Bridget would never stand for it. And he'd given the girl his word.

It was a puzzle, it was. If he sold the stallion, the girl would hate him. And if he didn't sell, he might be carted away to prison. Bridget could never run the stables alone. She knew enough—she knew as much, maybe more, than he did—but men wouldn't deal with a girl, even one who knew horses.

He straightened his shoulders. Maybe tomorrow's race would be different. Maybe this time he'd pick a winner. If he could get some money together to bet.

* * *

Three days later Andrew decided to go back to Durabian's. He wanted to tell the man to save the bay colt for him and to give Durabian a bank draft as a down payment. But it wasn't just because of that. He wanted to see the stallion—and his rider—again.

So he had Sable saddled, the stableboy sweating profusely as she shied about. Finally he had to go calm her himself. The ride into the country was pleasant in spite of the filly's skittishness. The trees were just coming into full bloom and everything had the fresh clean scent of spring, but even as he held the prancing filly in check, Andrew's thoughts raced ahead.

What was there about the strange girl that kept bringing her back into his mind? True, she had a kind of natural beauty, even in those awful male clothes, but he had seen—indeed, had been with—many beautiful women. Perhaps it was just her unusual occupation that intrigued him. And the stallion. That stallion would stay in anyone's mind.

It was midmorning when he turned Sable in at Durabian's gate. The Irishman came hurrying out to greet him. "Milord! I didn't expect to be seeing you so soon agin. And ye brought the filly. How grand!" He turned an expert's eye to the horse's flanks. "Aye, they weren't lying about the fine lines she has."

Andrew swung down and hooked the reins over his arm. "Yes, I'm quite pleased with her. I believe I made a good choice."

"That ye did, milord. That ye did!" Durabian ran a hand over the filly's gleaming withers. "Oh, she's a real beauty."

He turned toward the stables. "Bridget, girl, get out here and see his Lordship's filly. She's a rare sight."

The girl came out, wearing the same leather breeches and the same expression of cold disdain. But when she saw the filly, her expression changed. "Oh Papa! She's better even than they say. Look at her beautiful eyes!"

"Oh, you wonderful creature!" She drew the filly's head down and blew softly into her nostrils. When the horse whiffled in return and moved nose to nose with the girl, Andrew stiffened in amazement. Where was the high-strung creature who shied off at the mere approach of a stranger?

Bridget finished communing with the beast, who now stood docile, all her skittishness vanished. "She's a lovely horse," she said, her glowing eyes meeting his gaze. "You're a lucky man to have her."

"I know," Andrew said humbly. And basking in the light of her smile, he felt himself indeed fortunate.

"I hear she's a good racer," Bridget went on, laughter coming into her eyes. "Would you care to have a try against us?"

"No thank you," Andrew replied. "I'll happily concede that the stallion's the faster of the two."

She smiled again. Two smiles from her in as many minutes. How lucky could a man get?

"But perhaps you'd like to give her a run," he went on. "Alone, that is. She's feeling the fine weather and I kept her reined in on the way here."

Bridget started to reach for the reins then drew back. "I—I don't know, milord, she's your horse and—"

"I'd appreciate your doing it." He kept his voice normal. "Peter says you can handle any horse alive. And I believe it."

She didn't smile at him again. In fact, she lowered her head as though the compliment embarrassed her. But the mention of Peter seemed to have reassured her. "Well then, I'll just take her once around the track."

She led the horse off, and Andrew, watching her go, wondered how he could ever have thought this bewitching creature a boy.

The girl swung up, and Andrew swallowed. Peter was right about those infernal breeches. They made it deucedly hard for a man to think of their wearer as just another fellow.

"I can't believe it," he said to Durabian. "I had quite a time taming that filly. Took me days before I could get her confidence. And there your girl has her eating out of her hand in mere minutes."

Durabian chuckled. "She has a way with horses, Bridget does. They trust her right off. Too bad she ain't that good with people. She'd do better if she weren't so prickly."

The Irishman's smile turned into a frown and Andrew wondered idly what was bothering the man. Then his attention was again taken by the girl. She sat the filly like an extension of the animal, horse and rider moving together in one easy motion.

The beast pranced a little, eager to let loose, and the girl dropped a hand to her glossy neck, obviously soothing her.

"I can't get over the way she rides," Andrew said.

Durabian filled his pipe. "I had her in the saddle afore she could walk. Tied her on an old mare. Only way I could keep her from crawling round 'tween their hooves." He lit the pipe and took a big draw.

"She ain't never had no fear. Not even when she should've. I had a bad stallion once—meanest creature I ever seen. Kicked a couple stableboys just about into the next world. Bridget were about ten at the time. I come out one morning and seen her asleep in his stall." He shook his head. "The big devil like to kill me afore I could get her to wake up. Then she just looks at me, sober as a magistrate, and says, 'Papa, let me handle this.' And then she did."

"Where's the stallion now?" Andrew asked idly, his gaze on the girl and horse racing round the track in one smooth flowing motion.

"Sold him," Durabian said, "to yer friend Lord Peter, in fact."

For a moment Andrew forgot the girl and the horse. "You don't mean—"

"Aye," Durabian said. "I mean Diablo."

Andrew shook his head in bewilderment. "But that stallion's the best-mannered animal around."

"Course he is," Durabian said complacently. "Bridget had the fixing of him."

Andrew resumed watching the girl. "Perhaps I should give her Sable to train."

"As ye wish, milord. I don't know what it is, but Bridget's got the gift. She trusts horses and they trust her."

She came off the track then, swung down, and began walking the filly, speaking to her soothingly. At last, judging her cooled down sufficiently, she led her back to Andrew.

"She's a real beauty, milord. And well-trained, too." A

hint of mischief crossed the lovely face. "She's a little on the flighty side, but she's got a good heart. And she tells me you're a good master."

Andrew straightened. This was too much. "She what?"

Bridget laughed—pure tinkling notes of pleasure. "Really, milord, you ought to shut your mouth. With it hanging open like that you look rather foolish. The horse doesn't *talk* to me, not really. But all I have to do is look at her. Her mouth. Her coat. And her eyes. Her eyes are happy."

For once in his life Andrew was left speechless. He knew how to converse with elegant ladies and not so elegant ladies, though with the latter he didn't do much talking. But he had no idea how to speak with a girl who dressed like a man and yet looked more desirable than any woman he'd ever met. And whose only topic of conversation appeared to be the life and times of horses.

Chapter Three

Several weeks later Bridget paused in working a colt and frowned, uneasiness stirring the fine hairs on the back of her neck. It was a lovely morning, clear and bright, but something wasn't right in the stables. It wasn't with the horses, though. She could sense when something went wrong with one of them. This was something else, some uncomfortable presence close by.

The colt pricked up his ears, staring toward the lane. And then she saw why. Wichersham was riding up. His horse looked tired, poor creature, and though she couldn't see its eyes from this distance, she knew they would hold the beaten look she'd seen there before. Wichersham, for all his fine clothes and fancy manners, was a rotter. A bad master, a bad lord—a bad man.

Why had he come out to the stables today? Months ago Papa had taken one look at his mount's drooping ears and dragging tail and refused to sell him any animal in the stables. And that was before this business over Peter's vowels. Papa was fond of Peter. So was she. And neither of them thought it right for Wichersham to try to send Peter to debtor's prison.

She liked Peter's friend Haverly, too, though somehow not in the same way. He was fun like Peter, and she found she could joke with him and talk horses, but there was always that little something different that made it hard for her to entirely relax in his presence. And always in the back of her mind was the thought of that first day, the day that he'd touched her.

He hadn't touched her again. She was glad of that, of course, that was what she wanted—not to be touched again. Yet she felt a little shiver of curious disappointment. Had she imagined that strange feeling of excitement or would she feel it again if he—

"No!" Papa's voice carried clear across the paddock. She looked up and saw him glance hastily around. She couldn't hear any more, but she knew he was angry. The whole set of his body proclaimed it. He was angry at whatever Wichersham was saying to him.

But strain as she might, she couldn't hear another word of their conversation. She forced herself to concentrate instead on the colt she was training. Papa would deal with Wichersham. He knew the man. He wouldn't let him do them any harm.

Maybe Haverly would be coming round to the stables today. She hoped so. Strange, why should she think about him? And why should she get a picture in her mind of his lean dark face? She tried to push it away and concentrate on the colt—a frisky one who wanted off the long line to go play with his fellows in the pasture. "Not now, boy," she told him. "Work first, play later."

* * *

26

Across the paddock Victor Durabian swallowed a bitter curse. "You can't mean it." He kept his voice carefully down. Couldn't let Bridget know what was going on. He tried to think, to keep his voice reasonable. That was it. He had to reason with the man.

"Oh yes," Wichersham said, his eyes bright with evil intent. "I mean it. I have your vowels, you see. To the tune of a thousand pounds."

"A thousand—" Durabian lowered his voice still more. "Ye can't. I've never wagered with ye."

Wichersham shrugged and patted his coat pocket. "Nevertheless I have them. And I want the stallion."

"Ye can't—" Durabian swallowed hastily. He couldn't give the stallion to Wichersham. The horse wouldn't live long with the likes of him. He couldn't do that to any beast. And Bridget herself would die if anything happened to that horse.

"And if I don't pay—" He wouldn't concede that he couldn't. Not yet.

Wichersham shrugged. "You mean no money and no horse? I shouldn't think that would be wise. I hear debtor's prison isn't a particularly healthy place."

"I'll get the money." Durabian said it calmly, firmly.

But Wichersham just laughed. "There is another possibility," he said.

Durabian didn't allow himself to hope. Wichersham was enjoying this. And he was not the sort to give any man quarter. "And what is that?"

"Give me the girl instead."

Holy mother of God! "Bridget?" he asked, his heart gone cold, his voice carefully controlled. "Ye want me daughter?"

"Yes, your darling Bridget."

"Ye want to—" He couldn't bring himself to say the words.

"I want to *have* her." Wichersham smiled evilly. "For my paramour. For a while, at least."

Durabian bit his tongue and thrust his clenching fists deep into his pockets. He had to keep his temper under control. He needed all his wits about him. And knocking Wichersham to the earth and stomping on his face wouldn't change things a bit. The man would still hold his IOUs, and after a beating he'd be even more vindictive.

Wichersham chuckled, a sinister sound, turning Durabian's blood still colder. "I'm in no hurry. I'll give you a week to talk her into it." He sneered. "She'll do it to keep her papa out of prison. One week, and I'll be back."

Fighting the urge to throw something after him, Durabian watched the man go. The dirty, lily-livered bastard! He'd never give innocent Bridget to that evil-eyed rotter. At least he'd kept his temper. He'd bought them some time.

Time. But what could he do with it?

Andrew arrived at the Durabian stables in mid-afternoon. Something, he wasn't sure what, had prompted him to make the ride out to Pentonville. He told himself he was just going to see the bay colt, to check on his progress, but he knew there was more to it than that. He felt, somehow, that Bridget was in danger.

Durabian came out to greet him, pipe in hand. " 'Tis good to see ye, milord."

"Good to be here," Andrew returned. "Thought I'd

come have another look at the bay." Durabian didn't look quite up to snuff, but Andrew couldn't say exactly why.

Durabian nodded. "He's in the south paddock, milord." He hesitated, seemed about to say something more, then clamped his teeth on his pipe.

Leaning on the rail fence, they looked the colt over, a sturdy fellow, lively and quick. Andrew decided he'd been foolish. Nothing was wrong here.

And then Durabian spoke again. "Milord, I been thinking."

"Thinking?" Andrew repeated, turning.

"Aye, milord. Thinking 'bout a little race."

"A race?" Andrew felt ridiculous, repeating phrases like a child, but this had taken him completely by surprise.

"Aye. And a wager."

"I don't—" Andrew bit off the words. Durabian knew he didn't wager. There was something about the man's face, something that told him this wasn't just a race they were discussing. "What kind of wager?"

Durabian took a deep breath. Andrew heard it plainly and it told him this was serious business indeed.

"Well, it's like this, milord. Everyone's been talking 'bout Waterloo and yer filly Sable. And I been thinking, that is, mebbe we should have us a race—'tween the two of 'em."

"Go on," Andrew said, controlling his voice. "And the wager?"

Durabian shuffled his feet. "If Waterloo wins, I get Sable."

What kind of race was this? What was Durabian after? He had to know the stallion would win. "And if he loses?"

Durabian didn't meet his gaze. "If the stallion loses, you get him and . . . and Bridget to wife."

"Wife?" Andrew felt like he'd been dealt a sharp blow to the breadbasket. Surely he couldn't be hearing right.

"Aye. I'm worried 'bout the girl," Durabian said. "She needs a husband. And she ain't about to get one on her own. She likes ye well enough, I think. Ye could deal together."

Andrew tried to meet the man's eyes, but the Irishman kept his gaze on the ground. "Durabian, my friend," Andrew asked, "is something wrong? Are you ill?" What could the man be thinking? Bridget would never agree to wagering the stallion. And it looked like her father was in some kind of financial trouble.

Andrew thought fast. If he consented to the race, the stallion was sure to win it. Durabian would get the filly and—That was it. He could do that. "I'll do it on one condition."

Durabian's head snapped up; he looked startled but relieved. "An' what's that, milord?"

"That if the stallion wins, you let me buy the filly back. For five hundred pounds."

"But milord—"

"That way and no other," Andrew said. "And only if Bridget consents."

"She'll consent."

Maybe she would. After all, she knew the stallion and she knew the filly. He swallowed a sigh. This was a foolish thing he was doing. It would probably earn him the derision of the *ton*. But he was still going to do it. Durabian was obviously in some kind of trouble. And if Durabian was in trouble, the girl was too. A little ridicule meant nothing if he could help Bridget, innocent, fresh Bridget.

"Name the date," he said with resignation. "And the place. I'll be there."

"Two days from now," Durabian said. "At my track here."

"Done," Andrew said. "If Bridget agrees."

Bridget turned the colt into the paddock and tried not to hurry toward the fence where Papa and Lord Haverly stood talking. Since Wichersham had left, Papa had been behaving strangely. That awful man had said something to him, but she hadn't been able to find out what. When she'd asked if anything was wrong, Papa had just puffed away on his pipe and shaken his head.

Maybe his Lordship would be able to discover what was going on. She hoped so. She didn't like seeing Papa like this.

"Hello, Bridget," his Lordship said. "That colt you were working looks good."

"Thank you. He's a little on the frisky side, but he'll learn. What brings you out today?"

Haverly shrugged. "Nothing in particular. I just felt like it." He turned, directing a strange look at Papa.

Papa cleared his throat. "The stallion in good form?"

She snorted. "Of course he is. The best." What was wrong with Papa, asking such foolish questions?

"That's good," Papa said. "That's very good."

What was he talking about? And why did he look so strange? "Why?"

"His Lordship here—"

Haverly started, giving Papa another peculiar look.

"His Lordship here," Papa continued, "has made us a wager."

"Oh?" She looked from one man to the other. What was going on? "What kind of wager?"

"He thinks his filly Sable can beat the stallion."

How dare he! "You're joking! Beat Waterloo? Never!"

"Then you'll accept the race?"

This wasn't like Papa at all. "You mentioned a wager."

"If the stallion wins, his Lordship gives us Sable."

She stared. He couldn't mean—"*Gives* us!"

"Aye."

She looked at him suspiciously. "And if the filly wins?" She wouldn't, of course. No one could beat Waterloo.

"Then his Lordship gets the stallion."

For a moment she couldn't speak. "He gets Waterloo?"

"Aye, girl. But there's no need to fear. You said the stallion can't be beat."

His Lordship straightened, his gaze sharp. "Tell her the rest, Durabian. She must know it all."

Bridget swung round. "There's more?"

Papa smiled, a smile that didn't reach his eyes. "Aye, lass. If the filly wins, his Lordship gets the stallion and"—Durabian swallowed twice—"and yer hand in marriage."

Bridget reached out, grabbing a fence post for support. "Marriage! Papa, what kind of joke is this?"

Papa seemed to be avoiding her gaze. "No, girl, 'tis no joke. We thought 'twould liven the wager a bit. Ye ain't afraid of losing, are ye?"

"Of course not. But if we take his Lordship's filly—"

"I agree to the wager," his Lordship said stiffly, "and to the race. If *you* do. And your father has agreed to sell me the filly back—if the stallion wins."

"But he will," she cried. "You *know* he'll win." He did know it. She read it in his eyes. Then why was he willing to race?

"Do you agree?" he persisted. "Is it a race?"

She looked to Papa. "Papa, do you want—"

"Aye, girl. I want this race." He laughed, a hollow sound that made her instantly fearful. "This race'll draw a big crowd. Bring us plenty business."

Slowly Bridget lowered her gaze. She saw her fingers were gripping the fence post so tightly her knuckles had turned white. She unclenched her hand and opened her mouth, but nothing would come out. Her tongue felt numb, too swollen to work properly. How could they do such a thing, make such a wager without even consulting her?

She wet her dry lips. But she had always trusted Papa. "All right, Papa. If you want me to, I'll do it."

She risked one more look at his Lordship, but his face was closed, making him a stranger. Whatever this was— these two had set it up between them. There was more to it than a simple race, much more, but she knew men— they wouldn't tell her the truth. Protecting her, they called it, not realizing—or not caring—that not knowing the truth was no protection, no protection at all.

Chapter Four

The day of the race dawned bright and clear. Bridget, brushing the great stallion's glistening coat, sighed deeply. She was no closer to figuring out why Papa and his Lordship were doing this. But there was no need for her to be worrying about the wager. As fast as the perky little filly was, she could never beat the stallion. He *wouldn't* lose. She wouldn't have to marry his Lordship.

She paused, stopping the brush in mid-stroke. "Why?" she murmured to the horse. "Why are they doing this? I know something's wrong. Why don't they *tell me what it is?*"

The horse turned, nudging her with his nose. "Yes, I know," she murmured. "You love me. I love you, too."

She laughed, a laugh as hollow as Papa's had been when they told her about this race. "At least Papa put us in the same wager. If we lose, we go together."

What was she saying? Waterloo couldn't lose. He just couldn't.

Peering out the stable window, she swallowed hastily. The rail around the practice track was packed with people. Lords and their richly dressed ladies had driven out in their fancy carriages to watch. To watch *her*.

She glanced down at her breeches and boots, the same breeches and boots she always wore. She *had* put on a clean white shirt for the occasion. But she didn't look anything like those ladies out there, those ladies that would soon be staring at her.

The stallion nudged her, rubbing his nose against her sleeve. She had to remember these people meant nothing to her, nothing at all. She was doing this for Papa.

She straightened her shoulders, rubbed the stallion's nose, and said, "Let's go. They're waiting for us."

From his place by the fence, Andrew looked out over the noisy crowd. He hadn't cared much for Durabian talking the race up. But after what the man had said to Bridget, he couldn't tell him no. And the publicity would help the stables. Damnation, though, he was still puzzled by Durabian's desire to hold this race at all.

Well, it would be over soon. Sable would lose the race—he'd buy her back. And the story would spread around—Peter had already begun to do that—that Andrew had *expected* to lose the race and was willing to pay the price to see how well the filly could do.

His jockey, young Jackie, was one of the best riders around. Not as good as Bridget—there was no one as good with a horse as her—but good enough.

Andrew shifted irritably, wishing this silly charade were over. Why hadn't Durabian just asked him for a loan? And why that ridiculous addition to the wager—about him taking Bridget to wife? At least he'd insisted that they keep that part of the wager secret and the Irishman had agreed.

The girl, after her first look of shocked amazement, had seemed to take the wager in stride, acting rather like it was some huge joke. Still, he couldn't imagine her pleased with the prospect of marriage to a man she'd only known for a month.

A rather startling thought, that, and not one designed to raise his sense of self-importance. Although several young women of the *ton* had already made known to him their willingness, indeed, their extreme willingness, to become his wife, he hadn't really been thinking of marriage. He couldn't imagine Bridget as wife to any man. She was too set in her ways, too manlike in her behavior. Why, he could hardly imagine her wearing anything but breeches and boots. And to bring her into the *ton* as his wife . . .

He shook himself slightly. Of course that wouldn't be necessary. Plucky and fast as Sable was, the stallion was sure to win. Durabian wouldn't have made the wager otherwise.

Peter came hurrying up, his eyes bright with excitement. "I'm glad I've given up wagering," he said with a grin. "For if I did it still, I'd have to put my money on the girl. And you are my best friend."

Andrew managed to smile in return. "So would I. Have you dropped the hints as I asked?"

Peter nodded. "Oh yes. I told the Linden girl, the stickish one." He looked at his watch. "Told her five minutes ago. By now she's told her fat mama and at least half the crowd."

Andrew frowned. "And I look foolish."

"Not so. They all think you wonderfully eccentric."

Just what he needed! And the Lindens yet. Once they started talking, all London would be achatter.

"Is there much betting?"

Peter frowned. "Not really. The blacklegs aren't offering very good odds. The stallion's by far the favorite. I saw Wichersham." He grimaced. "I kept my distance, you can be sure. But I couldn't help hearing the fellow boast how he'd tame the animal if it were his." His eyes clouded over. "Makes a man's blood run cold just to hear him talk. And to think that he might have got ahold of Diablo—"

"He didn't," Andrew said firmly. "And he won't—as long as you leave off wagering."

"I *have*," Peter said vehemently, crossing his heart in the old childhood gesture of promise. "And I *will*. Look! Here she comes."

Bridget, her head held high, led the stallion toward the track where Jackie waited on the filly. Bridget was keeping her gaze away from the crowd, and she avoided his gaze, too. Lord! Andrew thought, he'd give a lot to know what the girl was thinking now.

Bridget didn't dare look at all the people. She kept her eyes straight ahead, feeling Waterloo's warm comforting breath against her ear.

We'll just trust Papa, she told herself. *That's what we'll do. He knows what he's doing.*

Waterloo nickered softly, sensing her uneasiness. He hadn't seemed quite himself this last hour, but then she wasn't herself either. He was probably picking up her feelings. That would explain it. But his ears weren't pricked as usual—and he didn't show his normal interest in the crowd.

Papa was waiting by Sable. He helped her mount Waterloo and then he whispered, "Don't worry, Bridget, 'twill all turn out for the best. Ye'll see."

That worried her almost as much as Waterloo's strange behavior. Usually before a race Papa was all smiles, jovial and happy. He should be that way today. After all, he knew Waterloo was bound to win. So why did he look so sober? So—

"We're ready to start this race," the appointed time-keeper shouted. "Horses to their places!"

Bridget kneed the stallion into line. He seemed sluggish, slow to respond to her commands. Was there something really wrong with him today? She started to turn back.

"Ready! Set! Go!"

Sable leaped forward, Waterloo right behind her. It was too late now to say anything. She had to race. Bridget leaned low, urging him on. "Come on, boy, you can do it!"

The first lap the horses kept even. The roaring of the crowd beat against her in great waves. Crouching over the horse, she tried to puzzle it out. Something was clearly wrong—Waterloo wasn't acting like himself. He should be ahead by now. Should she rein him in? Should she stop the race?

But that would make his Lordship the winner by default. And his winning would mean marriage to him and—She couldn't think of that. "Oh, please, Waterloo," she begged, "faster! You've got to beat her!"

But the second lap was no better than the first, and on

the third the filly pulled away from them! Bridget could feel Waterloo straining, trying his best, but it was as if some huge load was weighing him down, holding him back. No matter how the great horse tried, he could go no faster.

The filly won the race by a nose. Bridget could hardly believe it. She wanted to run somewhere, to hide her grief. Thank God these people didn't know about the second part of the wager. Maybe, maybe his Lordship would forget that part of it. But then she would lose Waterloo. And she wasn't sure she could bear that.

His Lordship wasn't a bad sort. She liked him better than any man she knew. Maybe being married wouldn't be so—

Papa was waiting when she dismounted. "Smile," he said, smiling himself, though a trifle strangely. "Trust me, Bridget, 'tis all fer the best."

She couldn't see how that could be, but she had always trusted him, and she could do no less now. "Yes, Papa," she said, and forced herself to smile.

Andrew stood stunned. Sable had won the race! But how could that be? Peter was tugging excitedly at his sleeve. "Come on! They're waiting."

Andrew, following through the crowd, tried to smile at the congratulations he was receiving. But he still couldn't believe it. Waterloo was his! And Bridget.

How was the girl going to react to this? Well, he'd find out after the crowd had dispersed. Then he'd offer to release her from that part of the wager. She was a proud one, too proud to be forced into marriage because of a horse race.

Still, though he might be able to prevail on the Irishman to forget the Bridget part of the wager, he knew Durabian would insist that the stallion was now Andrew's. Since that part of the wager was common knowledge, the man couldn't welsh on it without losing his reputation. They'd gotten themselves in a pretty tangle, and all because Andrew had wanted to help.

Finally the crowd was gone. Andrew had sent Peter on, waiting alone. He wanted to put the girl's mind to rest, but he couldn't do it when someone might overhear. Besides, she'd avoided him after the race, walking the stallion up and down to cool him off and then taking him back to the stable.

As the last carriage headed back toward London, Durabian came toward him. Now, Andrew thought, tell him right away. "We'll forget the part about the girl," he said with no preliminaries. "It isn't—"

"Ye can't!" Durabian glanced around almost fearfully. "Ye've got to take her!" He grabbed Andrew by the arm, his fingers tightening almost painfully. "Please, milord, I got me reasons—good 'uns. Bridget, she's got to be safe, too."

Andrew read the fear in the old man's eyes. Safe from what? There was something awfully wrong here. "But I—"

"Please, milord. I'm counting on ye. And do it quick! Get a special license and make her legally yer wife. Right off!"

"But man, she'll hate me."

Durabian shook his head. "She might be a little tetchy

at first, but she'll tame down. Please, milord, ye've got to take her. I'm begging it of ye."

"But—"

"Hush! Here she comes."

As she went toward them, Bridget risked a glance at his Lordship's face. He looked almost as bad as she felt. Probably he didn't want the marriage either. Maybe—

"His Lordship'll pick up the horse after the wedding," Papa said before she could open her mouth.

"After?" Her heart fell. So they meant to go through with it.

"Aye. He's getting a special license. So ye'll be wed tomorrow."

"We won't be calling the banns?" How could they rush her like this? She'd thought she would have at least a few weeks to get used to the idea.

"No," Papa said. "It'll be by special license. Ain't that right, yer Lordship?"

Haverly looked uncomfortable. "Yes, that seems best." He looked at her, meeting her eyes squarely. "I'm sorry about this unseemly haste, Bridget, but it does appear best to get the deed done. Afterwards you and Waterloo can come live with me."

She nodded. It was like a dream, a bad dream.

"I'll be a good husband to you, Bridget, I promise. And I'll leave the horse in your hands."

She almost broke then, fighting hard to control her tears. It wasn't fair that men should have the running of a woman's life. Not fair at all. Still, his Lordship was being kind. Some men would have taken the stallion for their own. She swallowed over the lump in her throat. "Thank you, milord."

"Andrew," he said, the ghost of a smile tugging at his lips. "My name is Andrew. Please call me by it."

Some minutes later Andrew told his driver, "Home," and leaned back in his carriage. He could hardly believe any of this was happening. In the space of a few minutes he'd acquired a superb stallion and a prospective wife. And he still wasn't sure how it had happened.

Why had Durabian been so emphatic about his taking Bridget to wife? It had seemed as though the man thought some harm would come to her if he didn't get her married off immediately. But what harm? Certainly Durabian was man enough to protect her from anyone, except possibly the Prince Regent. And he couldn't imagine Prinny, whose current taste ran to grandmothers, wanting to bother with Bridget.

Well, whatever his reason, Durabian's urgency was clear. His haste for the wedding showed that. The poor girl should have been given some weeks to prepare, but instead he had conceded to her father's evident apprehension and agreed to this imminent marriage.

Tomorrow at this time Bridget would be his wife—and a lady. Lord, how the *ton* would gossip then! Thank goodness they'd kept that part of the wager secret. The *ton* would think him even more eccentric, but the onus would fall on him, not Bridget. Lords had been known to marry commoners before, all sorts of commoners. So that was nothing new.

He shook his head. He had a great deal to do. Mrs. Purvey would have to set her staff to work preparing the room adjoining his. It was decorated in yellow and hardly a suitable foil for an occupant of Bridget's coloring, but she should have a chamber of her own. Later he would have it redecorated in more complementary shades. Or better yet, give the redoing of it into her hands.

Good grief! As soon as he reached the city, he must go directly to the dressmaker's. The girl would need a gown to be wed in—something simple but elegant, something white.

The thought gave him pause. Was Bridget the innocent she appeared to be? He frowned. He'd had ample experience with women, but none of it had prepared him for a woman like Bridget. She was an unknown quantity—he didn't know how to handle her. Well, he'd get to that later.

Let's see. She'd definitely need clothes. She probably only owned one gown, if that, so she'd need the whole array—morning dresses, walking dresses, evening dresses, a riding habit. She'd need boots and slippers, too. And bonnets and gloves. All the little frewfraws that delighted feminine hearts.

Thank goodness she spoke well: the effect, no doubt, of her mama's books—over which her father said she pored daily—a good ear for language, and the efforts of the teacher Durabian had hired for her. But perhaps he should engage a dancing master. The rest he could teach her himself—the proper eating utensil, the proper reply to introductions, the proper curtsy.

He frowned. He liked the old Bridget. She had a rough, untutored honesty, a freshness that appealed to him. What would she be like when she lost that freshness? When she became like the other ladies in the *ton?*

He sighed. It was next to impossible to imagine Bridget as a lady at all. But he could imagine her in the room next to his, even in his bed. He gave himself up to thinking about the pleasanter aspects of this marriage.

Chapter Five

The next day Bridget stood before the vicar. Haverly—
no, she was supposed to call him Andrew now—stood at
her side. She felt like some other woman, not herself at all.
For one thing this gauzy white gown he'd given her to be
married in seemed almost indecent after the safety of her
familiar leather breeches. And the flimsy little satin slippers and thin stockings were practically useless for keeping her feet warm. The patterned Indian shawl was pretty
and it did help to keep her from catching a chill, but a
jacket would have been much better. Much more sensible, too. It was hard to see how ladies could do anything
at all wearing these peculiar clothes, clothes that made it
practically impossible to move.

Of course, Mama had been a lady. A beautiful lady,
Papa said, and kind, too.

Bridget sighed. *She* wasn't beautiful—or kind. Except to
animals. Too bad she wasn't a horse. She'd make a good
mare—and if Hav—if Andrew were a stallion, maybe
they could—

The vicar paused in the words he was saying, words

about love and honor. How did they expect her to love a man she'd only known a month? What *was* love anyway? Certainly not something that could be won in a wager.

She glanced sideways at the man who would soon be her husband. She supposed it was honor that made him go ahead with this marriage. He had given his word and he would stand by it. She liked that about him—that he was an honorable man.

And his looks weren't bad. He looked quite handsome today, but she liked him better in the clothes he usually wore to the stable—tan buckskins and shining top boots, a white cravat and a coat of blue superfine. The fancy black clothes he had on today made him even more the stranger to her.

Papa looked strange, too, in the best clothes which he hardly ever wore. But he looked happy, happier than either of them. For some reason known only to him, Papa wanted her married to Andrew. It was very odd. He'd never wanted her married before. Why he should want it now?

She pulled her attention back to the vicar. He had reached the point where *she* was supposed to speak. She said the proper words and soon the ceremony was over. She was Andrew's wife. He offered her his arm, and Papa and Peter followed them down the aisle.

Thank goodness there were no other spectators; no one but Papa and Peter had witnessed this strange marriage.

Outside the church, Andrew shook Durabian's hand. "The situation is unusual," he said, his face grave. "But I want you to know that I'll do my best to make Bridget happy."

Papa smiled. "I know ye will," he said. "Else I'd not have given her into yer keeping."

What was Papa talking about now? She didn't need to be in anyone's keeping. She was perfectly capable of taking care of herself—if men would only recognize it. But of course they didn't. They had to go on thinking that *they* were the strong ones—in charge of everything, knowing everything, when most of the time they knew very little.

Andrew's carriage was waiting, the driver holding open the door for them.

"Well," Papa said, his voice turning hoarse. "Ye go along now and be happy."

Bridget nodded. The lump in her throat had grown too big for talking over.

Andrew shook Durabian's hand again. "I'll send for the stallion in the morning," he went on. "If that's agreeable."

"The sooner the better," Papa said cheerfully. "I know Bridget'll be wanting him close at hand. Him being like her baby and all."

For the first time it struck her that Papa would be left alone. "Oh, Papa!" she cried, taking a step toward him. "I don't want to leave you!"

He grabbed her in a warm comforting hug. "Remember," he whispered in her ear, " 'tis all fer the best now."

She blinked back her tears. "Yes, Papa." Why did she have this silly desire to cry? She could come out to the stables every day if she wanted. She was a lady now. And ladies did as they pleased.

"I'll send the carriage out tomorrow," Andrew said, "when the groom comes for the stallion. I'm sure Bridget has some things she'll want besides what she's bringing along with her today. Her mother's books and such."

She nodded. "I have them all ready." No need to tell them that under the books she'd packed her breeches and boots. At least she'd have Waterloo—she'd be able to ride. Perhaps being a lady wouldn't be so bad. And it was what Papa wanted.

A while later Bridget wasn't so sure. The drive back to London seemed to be taking forever. She was bounced and jiggled around on the seat. Hav—Andrew must have the best carriage available, but riding in it was nothing at all like riding a horse. She knew what the trouble was— there was no connection between her and the animals pulling the carriage. Perhaps . . . She turned to the man beside her. "Andrew, could I drive the carriage?"

The look he gave her was shocked, but his voice was even. "I'm afraid not, my dear." He glanced down at her fancy clothes. "You're not really dressed for it anyway."

"That's unfair," she cried, unable to stop herself. "I didn't ask for these clothes. I didn't ask to marry you!"

Instead of getting angry, he put on a look of patience, like she was some skittish filly who needed a firm hand. "I know that, Bridget. But you did agree to it." He heaved a big sigh. "The deed is done. So why don't we make the best of it?"

He turned on the squabs, looking her squarely in the eyes. "You're a lady now, and—"

"I don't *want* to be a lady! I want to be the Bridget I've always been!"

He heaved another, even greater, sigh. She heard it

48

clearly, even over the sounds of the horses' passage along the road.

"Nevertheless," he said in that calm soothing voice she was beginning to loathe, "you *are* a lady. You are the Marchioness of Haverly."

She glared at him. "How can I be a marchioness? I don't know anything about being a lady." She looked down at the gown—her wedding gown. "Except that they wear these stupid clothes. I can't see how they can get any work done in these things. I really can't."

"Ladies don't work," Andrew said, his lips twitching as though he were trying not to smile. "They paint in watercolors, they play the pianoforte, they sing a little, and they do needlepoint."

This was ridiculous. "Lord love a duck! That's no life at all."

Andrew was looking more and more pained, but he still held to his patience, artificial though she could tell it was. "Most ladies are quite content with their lives," he went on.

She barely kept herself from voicing her contempt for such emptiness. "Do they ever go outside? Do they get to ride?"

"Oh yes." He seemed pleased to be able to tell her that. "A few even drive carriages. Female Jehus, we call them." He frowned. "You'll have Waterloo, and you can ride all you please, so I hope you won't feel it necessary to drive a carriage, too."

Bridget managed a smile. It was time to remember that this man was her husband, that in the eyes of the law he was her legal master. They would probably have a lot of disagreements as it was. It wasn't smart to raise his hackles over something silly, something that meant so little to her.

"I won't drive," she said. "I promise. I was just feeling restless. Usually by this time of day I've been working the horses for hours." She squirmed on the hard seat. "I'm not used to sitting still—or riding in a carriage."

"I think I understand," he said, patting her hand. She felt a little twinge of that excitement she'd felt that first time he touched her. Would she feel it every time he touched her?

He smiled at her, a smile that made him look more like the man she knew. "Why don't you sit back now and relax a bit? It's a while yet till we reach home."

I've left my home, she thought, *and my father,* but she didn't say it aloud. Andrew was doing the best he could. After all, he couldn't help it that he was a lord. They *were* married and they would have to learn to deal together. Perhaps after tonight . . .

She had no experience of men, but she understood the act of consummation. She'd seen horses mate. Of course, Papa had said that for people, mating was more gentle, more tender. And he'd assured her that she'd learn to like it.

She sighed and closed her eyes. She'd always trusted Papa—all her nineteen years. He was her teacher, her best friend, too. And since he'd told her Mama had liked it—well, he'd sort of told her that—she knew she would like it, too.

On the squabs next to her, Andrew frowned. This marriage looked to be more difficult than he'd thought. The fashionable clothes had not made a lady out of Bridget. In sober fact, she looked odd in them. And she walked as though she still wore boots, which made her look odder still. She'd stripped off her gloves the moment they'd settled in the carriage, throwing them and her bonnet on the opposite seat. Her hands and arms were brown from the sun—her face, too. And a bridge of freckles marched across her nose.

She looked like a child, a ragamuffin child, washed and dressed up in a lady's clothes. When he let his gaze wander lower, though, to the swell of bosom that even the shawl didn't hide, he knew better. This was no child sitting here beside him. This was a woman—a full-grown woman.

He wasn't at all sure that marrying her had been wise—several times he'd almost decided to call the wedding off. But that look of desperate urgency in Durabian's eyes had made him go ahead with it. Durabian wanted this marriage, that much was clearly evident. And that meant—it must mean—that Bridget was in some kind of danger, danger from which only marriage to him would save her.

He was flattered Durabian thought him a suitable husband for Bridget—he knew how much the man loved the girl—but he wasn't at all sure he was up to being husband to such a creature.

Tonight, for example, should he—? He found the thought was bringing the blood to his face and heating his body in a very disconcerting way.

He shifted his thoughts. The more he considered it, the more he was forced to conclude that Durabian's action in pushing this marriage on him was very odd. And, given the importance he attached to having Bridget safely married, why had Durabian hung the marriage on a wager that he knew had little hope of being won? Unless—

Andrew stifled a sigh. As soon as he reached home, he'd have to send a man to look into Durabian's affairs. Something was rotten, and it wasn't in Denmark.

They reached London in midafternoon. Bridget had been alert for some time, taking in the sights around her. The city was a strange place, full of loud dirty people, half of them wanting to sell something to you, the other half wanting to steal something from you. She'd been to the city before a few times when Papa went in to Tattersall's to look at the horses. But she hadn't liked London then and she didn't like it now. She much preferred the company of horses, the clean fresh air of the country, and the quiet of fields and stables.

But they went on through the noisy part of the city, eventually coming to quieter neighborhoods. She looked around her with interest. Strange that such wealthy lords and ladies should live in houses all squashed up together. They were nice-looking houses, of course, rich-looking, and she supposed with so many people about in a city, a man, even a lord like Andrew, couldn't take up too much space. Still and all, she much preferred the country. Papa's cottage might be small, but at least there a person had room to move around, room to breathe.

The carriage came to a halt in front of one of the great houses. "We're home," Andrew said.

He helped her out of the carriage and led her up the walk and in the front door, past the butler, to where the household staff stood waiting in a long line. Lord! Why did one man need so many people to take care of him?

Drawing her arm through his, Andrew took her down the line, introducing each servant in turn. "And this," he said with a smile to the round little woman who stood apart, "this is Mrs. Purvey, the housekeeper. If you need anything, you have only to ask her."

Bridget nodded. She liked the look of the woman, but she wasn't sure how a lady would behave to a housekeeper. "Thank you," she said finally. "I'll do that."

Then he led her upstairs to the yellowest room she'd ever seen, all furnished with fancy gilt furniture that looked too fragile to sit on and a great satin-covered bed big enough to hold the stallion—and a filly, too. She swallowed a sigh. She missed Waterloo already.

"Pay no attention to the way the room is done," Andrew said. "I know this isn't the proper color for you. You can redo the room however you please." He motioned toward another door. "That door connects to my chamber."

She stared at him, her heart pounding. She knew little about marriage, it was true, but she knew one thing. Married people shared a bed—and this one was certainly big enough to share.

"We don't—" she began, unsure how to ask, "sleep together? In the same bed?"

A funny look crossed his face. "We may. But it's customary for a lady to have her own boudoir."

Stupid, that's what it was. Wasting all this space just for sleeping. Rich people didn't seem to have much sense.

"I'll leave you now," Andrew said, "to freshen up." He indicated the pitcher and basin, the stack of fresh linen towels. "And perhaps you'd like to rest a little before dinner."

Rest! Good grief, that's all she'd *been* doing. But she bit her tongue and didn't say so.

"I'll send up a girl to help you dress."

"I can dress myself," she pointed out, turning away from a vanity table that had obviously just been brought into the room. "I've done it all my life. Besides, this is the only decent gown I've got."

He frowned. "That's right. But we'll fix that tomorrow. We'll go to Bond Street and get you all fitted out."

"Can't you do that kind of thing without me?" she asked. "I want to go see Papa."

Andrew took both her hands in his, holding them tightly. "Bridget, listen to me. We both know your Papa wanted this marriage. Don't we?"

She nodded. She wouldn't have gone through with it otherwise.

"Do you know why?"

That made her curious. "No, do you?"

"No," Andrew said, "except that I feel that he was afraid of something. Afraid for you. And until we find out what that something is, perhaps you'd better stay away from the stables."

She knew he made sense but she still had to protest. "But Papa, and Waterloo?"

"I'll send out for the stallion just as I promised—and for your other things. Just don't go out there. For now. Give me—let's say, give me three days to look into this thing, to find out what's going on. Just three days. Then I'll take you out there myself." He looked deep into her eyes. "Will you give me your word?"

She swallowed over the hard lump in her throat. Three days seemed like forever. And she never broke her word.

But Andrew was right. She knew something was wrong with Papa, something was very wrong. "All right," she said. "You have my word. But in three days we'll go together to see Papa."

He smiled at her then, squeezing her hands and releasing them quickly. "In three days. You have my word on it."

Chapter Six

Dinner was a dismal affair. Bridget missed Papa so much that even the distraction of new foods and the fancy furnishings in Andrew's great dining room couldn't make her feel better. And the way rich people ate—so much food and so many different utensils to eat it with—was ridiculous. Who ever heard of a special spoon just to eat soup? And there was enough food in the dishes the footman offered her to fill the stomachs of several country families.

She was going to ask Andrew about such waste. Why did the rich have such peculiar habits? Didn't they think about other people at all? But Andrew seemed distracted, hardly talking. The meal was scarcely over before the butler Purvey appeared to announce, "Blackburn to see you, milord." And Andrew excused himself and went off into his study with the stranger.

She wandered around the library, admiring all the books that were now hers to read—if she wanted to. She would read them someday, but she couldn't settle down tonight. She couldn't sit still, let alone concentrate on reading anything.

Tonight, tonight was her wedding night. And in spite of all she knew and all Papa had said about the naturalness of the marriage act, she was nervous about it. She paced the Persian carpet. Back and forth, back and forth, in those flimsy satin slippers that were hardly better than nothing at all.

She paused, looking up at the landscape over the mantel. Turner, she read the painter's name in the corner. How did the man get sunshine to look so very real? It was amazing what he could do with a little paint.

But in a moment she turned away. Why didn't Andrew finish his business with that stranger and come to her? All this waiting was quite nerve-wracking.

What was Papa doing now, eating his supper alone? And Waterloo, was he fretting in his stall because she wasn't there to care for him? Poor Waterloo. He wouldn't understand any of this. But then, neither did she. Not really.

Three days. Why had she promised Andrew she'd wait three whole days before she went back to Papa's? Three days seemed like forever. She wanted to see Papa now.

From the doorway of his study, Andrew watched Blackburn go down the hall toward the front of the house. Blackburn was a good man, thorough and fast, one of the best. Of course, as he'd pointed out, the information hadn't been that hard to find.

Andrew sighed. Too bad he hadn't thought to look into Durabian's affairs *before* the wedding. So simple a matter could have been easily handled. Good grief, why hadn't the man just asked him for the money?

He turned. Bridget would be waiting for him in the library, Bridget his new wife. Lord! What a bumble broth they were all in!

The library door opened. "Andrew?" she called, her voice anxious. "Has your visitor left?"

"Yes," he replied. "I'll be there directly." He turned back into the study, trying to gain a little time. He had to have a moment to think this thing through. Could he keep what he'd discovered from her? Probably not. He heaved a great sigh. There was no use in lying. He would have to tell Bridget the truth. At least part of it.

He straightened his shoulders and headed down the hall. Experience had taught him that it was best not to postpone difficult things—putting them off only made them more difficult.

When he opened the library door, Bridget turned quickly, her lovely face showing anxiety. "Was it anything important?" she asked. "Did you find out something about Papa?"

Andrew crossed the room to her and took her hands. "Come, sit on the sofa beside me and I'll tell you what I know."

She came, her face wreathed in worry, and settled anxiously beside him. "Tell me, Andrew, is it something terrible?"

"It will be all right," he promised, wishing he didn't have to tell her at all. "It's not that serious."

"For mercy's sake," she cried, clutching at his sleeve with panicky fingers, "tell me!"

"He's in debt," Andrew said. "Your father owes quite a bit of money. IOUs from wagers he made on races."

Bridget frowned. "I know he wagered a lot—and often. I tried to stop him. I talked and talked to him, but it did no good. He had to wager, it seemed."

Tears stood in her lovely eyes. Without much thought, he put an arm around her shoulders, drew her close against his side, holding her as he would have held a child. "It'll be all right," he repeated. "I promise."

She pulled out a handkerchief, one of the new ones he'd sent her with the gown, and dabbed at her eyes. "How much?" she asked. "How much does Papa owe?"

He was almost afraid to tell her. The man really had been foolish to risk so much. "A thousand pounds."

"A thousand—" She pulled away, her face white with shock. "Oh no! He can't pay that. I know he can't. They'll be after him! They'll send him—" She swallowed a sob. "They'll send him to debtor's prison." She covered her face with her hands. "Oh no! Poor Papa."

He patted her shoulder. "Bridget, don't cry. I won't let that happen. I'll pay his debts."

She looked at him, her eyes wide. "Really, you would do that? A thousand pounds?"

"Of course," he said. "I'll take care of it first thing in the morning."

"Oh, thank you!" She wiped at her eyes again, then stiffened. "Andrew, is that it? Is that why Papa made the wager?"

"I believe so," he said, not voicing his other suspicions. It was better to keep Wichersham's name from her. If she knew he was responsible, she would want to tell the man off. And the thought of her being anywhere near Wicher-

sham unsettled his stomach, filling him with a vague uneasiness. "Your father couldn't pay his debts and he
feared he'd be sent to debtor's prison."

"And he wanted me to be safe."

Andrew nodded. "Safe with me."

She gave him an unfathomable look. "And I am. I'm
safe."

Bridget wiped again at her eyes with that bit of lacy
linen ladies called a handkerchief. It was stupid to act like
a waterworks, dripping tears all over Andrew like some
kind of baby. But why, oh why, had Papa done such a
terrible thing?

Wagering was bad enough, but a thousand pounds! He
could lose the stables—the whole stables. And all the
horses that were her friends.

She swallowed hastily. But not Waterloo. Papa had
seen to it that the stallion was safe. Just as he'd made sure
she was safe. At least he'd done that much.

If only they'd known in time. Andrew was looking at
her so strangely. Probably he was thinking the same thing
she was. That this marriage of theirs was a mistake. They
could have prevented it. Could he—Would he have it
annulled?

He was frowning now, his handsome face screwed up
in a grimace. "Don't worry, Bridget," he said. "Please
don't worry. Your father will be all right. You have my
word on it."

"Thank you," she said, taking comfort from his words,
"and tomorrow we can go see Papa!"

Andrew hesitated. "We must wait till the debt is paid.
Give me a day for that."

She wanted to see Papa, to know that he was safe, but

she knew Andrew was right. They had better wait. "All right."

Andrew got to his feet and helped her up. "Come, Bridget, it's late. It's time we went up to bed."

She swallowed hastily. He meant to do it, then, to go on with the marriage. She felt something oddly like relief, but that couldn't be right. After all, she hadn't really wanted this marriage. She'd only done it to please Papa.

Andrew tucked her arm through his and led her toward the stairs. "We'll both be the better for a good night's rest," he said as they ascended.

She hardly heard what he was saying for thinking that in her room, spread across the yellow satin bedcover, and looking completely out of place there, lay her faded flannel nightdress. Soon she would put on that nightdress and Andrew would—

He opened the door and motioned her into the room. From the bed the nightdress seemed to call out to her, to shine like a bright beacon, a beacon she'd like to put out.

Andrew looked around the room. "I think you have everything you'll need. If not, add it to our list for tomorrow."

He drew her to him, and her heart jumped up in her throat, beating there frantically. He put his arms around her, in a hug much like Papa might have given her, only this hug made her feel quite different, excited and comforted at the same time—a very strange sensation, but pleasant enough.

Then he held her off a little, put a kiss on her forehead, and said, "Sleep well, now. I'll see you in the morning."

And he went out, through the connecting door to his

own chamber. She stood staring after him, unable to believe what she was feeling.

Andrew didn't want her. Maybe he even meant to get an annulment that would free her to go home to Papa.

She turned away, hastily unfastening her gown. But wait, he said he would pay Papa's debts, keep him from prison, so . . . So nothing, she told herself crossly, yanking her nightdress down over her head. So that didn't mean one thing or another about their marriage.

It was the most irritating thing imaginable. She didn't *want* to be married to Andrew. She wanted to be at home with Papa. But the prospect of being sent back to him left her feeling strangely disappointed.

Well, Andrew was right about one thing. It had been a long day. And she needed some sleep.

In the adjoining chamber Andrew prepared for bed. What a day this had been! He climbed between the cold sheets and lay, staring up into the darkness. He supposed he'd been right to tell Bridget about her father's debts. And right, too, he thought, in withholding the name of the man who held those notes. No wonder Durabian had panicked, been frantic to get Bridget safely married and the stallion out of his stables.

It was Wichersham who held the notes, Wichersham who had no qualms about ruining man, woman, or child. Or animal, as far that went. Well, old Durabian had outfoxed him. It appeared fairly certain that the Irishman had meant for Waterloo to lose the race. But how had he accomplished it?

Andrew had heard of races in which the rider held the horse back. Bridget! Waterloo loved her. He would obey

62

any command she gave him. Had she kept the horse from winning?

He supposed it was possible. But it was hard to imagine Bridget being party to any such plan. She was too honest, too proud of the stallion, to resort to trickery.

He sighed. There was no way to tell for sure. Asking would not assure him the truth, and it might insult her. Besides, even if he found that she *had* cheated, what good would the knowledge do him? He and Bridget were truly married—in the eyes of the church, and in his own. They'd do better just to make the best of it.

Besides, he couldn't believe Bridget had been guilty of anything shady. He shifted in the cold bed. Should he have stayed with her tonight? He'd wanted to, but she'd looked so exhausted that he hadn't the heart to make any more demands on her. But tomorrow night—

He smiled and willed himself to relax. Marriage to Bridget might not be half bad. If nothing else, it was sure to be interesting.

Chapter Seven

Bridget woke the next morning with a sense of apprehension. Something wasn't right, but at first she was too sleepy to remember what that something was. And then she remembered. Papa! Papa owed that awful amount of money. She jumped from the bed, washed quickly, and hurried into her clothes. She had to see Andrew, to find out what he had done about it.

The dining room was empty, but there was food, far too much food, of course, on the sideboard. And a footman appeared right away to inquire if she wanted anything else.

She frowned. "Where is his Lordship?" she asked. "Has he had breakfast yet?"

"Oh yes, milady," the footman replied. "He came down early and went out."

Good! Bridget slowly filled her plate. Andrew was out keeping his word. When he came back, he'd have Papa's debts paid. The thought gave her comfort and she enjoyed the food, eating far more than she was used to, but it seemed a shame to waste it—bacon, eggs, ham, kippers, and muffins with butter and apricot marmalade. And a great pot of tea to wash it all down.

She had just finished when Andrew came striding in. "Good morning," he said. "You'll be glad to know your father's safe. I sent my factor to take care of his debts. By now it's all done."

She smiled, her heart feeling a million times lighter. "Good. Then we can ride out to see him."

But Andrew frowned, looking very fatherish. "Bridget, I think we'd better wait till tomorrow to go out there. We've a lot to do today. You need everything, you know—gowns and petticoats, shoes and stockings, shawls and bonnets, and all the other things ladies wear."

"But I don't need anything," she protested. "My regular clothes will do fine."

"They will not do fine," he replied, his face turning so stern she knew she'd made a serious mistake. "You're a lady now," he went on, "and you must act like one."

Why must he be so autocratic? And why must ladies act differently than ordinary people? "But I want to ride."

Andrew sighed heavily, like Papa when she wanted to do something he disapproved of. "Bridget, you will ride. We'll order you a habit. Something in forest green, perhaps, to go with your coloring. And riding boots, new ones. You'll see. You'll like having new gowns."

She didn't protest anymore. She knew that look on a man's face. If *he* said she would like something, then it was smartest to agree with him, even if *she* knew she wouldn't. After all, how long could a man like Andrew occupy himself with feminine frivolities? He'd soon tire of this shopping business and then she'd be free to do as she pleased. And when she *was* free, she'd jump into her old clothes and have a good ride on Waterloo—a good long ride.

"Very well," she said, trying to smile pleasantly. "But you will send for Waterloo, won't you? Like you promised? And for my boxes?"

"Of course," he said. "They should be here by the time we return."

Shopping with Bridget had turned out to be much more than he'd bargained for, Andrew thought some hours later as they emerged from a shop on Bond Street. He looked around for the carriage: it was time to go home. Bridget was polite enough—none of those icy freezing looks she'd given him that first day at the stables—but she seemed almost not to be there with him, her mind miles away—with the stallion, no doubt. He would never have believed it if he hadn't seen it for himself, but the chit actually *didn't* care about clothes. She was the first female he'd ever known who would rather talk about horseflesh than about fashion.

Still, he had persisted in his efforts—she was his wife, after all, and if he meant to take her about in society, she would have to be properly dressed—and he was confident she now had everything she would need, even to half a dozen fine linen nightdresses embroidered with Belgian lace. He smiled, remembering the flush that had crossed her cheeks when they were purchasing them. In some things she was such an innocent. He would have much to teach her. And he meant to start tonight.

"Andrew," she said, tugging on his arm. "Do you know those ladies there—the ones across the street? I believe they're waving at you."

"Across the—Damnation! Your pardon, Bridget." He hadn't meant to use such harsh language in front of her, but the word had just slipped out. Still, he could certainly be pardoned for it, as it was the Lindens that stood across the street—Lady Linden in a puce gown of vast proportions that still barely managed to cover her more than ample charms, and her daughter Martine, straight as the mother was round. But it wasn't their looks that made him exclaim in exasperation, though they made quite a peculiar pair, but their reputations.

Scandalmongers par excellence, the Lindens were known over all of London. Any hint of scandal, any *on-dit*, was grist for their gossip mill, bruited about the city by mother and daughter, as fast as their carriage could convey their bodies and their tongues could wag the tales out.

Well, it was too late to avoid them now, too late to pretend he hadn't seen them over there. Lady Linden was already hurrying the stickish daughter toward him, both of them grinning like carnivorous beasts about to dine on unsuspecting prey. Poor Bridget, she'd have little chance against those two.

"Lord Haverly," Lady Linden cooed, grabbing his arm in a ferocious grip as though he meant to run off.

"Lady Linden," he muttered, easing his arm free, though with difficulty, and wishing himself somewhere else, anywhere else. "And Miss Linden. Good day to you both."

Lady Linden didn't bother with the amenities. "Who *is* this lovely young thing?" she asked, her eyes gleaming with barely concealed curiosity.

"This," he said, wishing momentarily that there were witnesses present to see the Lindens' expressions when he imparted his shocking news, "this is my lady wife, Bridget, the Marchioness of Haverly."

Lady Linden actually swayed and clutched at her daughter. "Wife! Lord Haverly, you say wife?"

"Indeed, I do," he replied, smiling grimly. "My wife. And now if you'll excuse us . . ."

"I know you!" Miss Linden shrilled, her voice calculated to draw all eyes in their direction. Her thin nose quivered ecstatically, the gossip hound hot on the scent. "I saw you at the race several days past. You're that Durabian girl, the one whose father trains horses!"

Andrew, risking an apprehensive look at Bridget, found himself surprised and had hard work to contain his sudden laughter. His worry for her had been needless. His innocent Bridget had turned into the frostiest of ladies. "Yes, Miss . . . ?" Why did he feel she was only pretending to forget Miss Linden's name? "You're quite right. But *I* train horses also." She glanced at Andrew. "Or I have trained them. But now I am Andrew's wife. As he says, Lady Haverly."

"Well, I never!" Miss Linden stared aghast, her thin mouth hanging open in a most unattractive manner.

"Really, Lord Haverly," Lady Linden protested, her round cheeks wrinkling in dismay. "To marry such—"

"Yes, she is lovely." He cut the mother off before she could offend Bridget further. From the look of her, his wife's Irish temper was on the rise. And Bond Street was not the place for a scene. The *ton* would have more than enough to talk about as it was. "If you'll excuse us," he went on, "we've just finished a long day's shopping and we're most anxious to get home with our packages."

Lady Linden looked about, almost wildly. No doubt

she was calculating where to find the nearest ear, an ear into which to pour this choicest of *on-dits*. "Of course, Lord Haverly, of course," she muttered, drawing the girl away with her. "Shut your mouth, Martine," he heard her command sharply, and then they were out of earshot.

He turned to Bridget. "Shall we go home?"

"Yes," she agreed, raising an eyebrow. "And on the way perhaps you can tell me about those two—*ladies*. I never knew ladies were supposed to ask such rude questions."

He laughed, relief flooding through him. It looked like Bridget was going to handle society much better than he'd expected. "I'll do that," he promised, "though I don't think you're going to like what you hear."

By the time they reached the house, Bridget had decided that Andrew was right. The Lindens sounded—and behaved—like perfectly horrible people and she wanted nothing more to do with them.

What she did want was a ride. So when Andrew directed the butler to have their purchases taken up to her room, she turned to him. "Is Waterloo in the stable now? Can we go see him? Please, Andrew?"

Andrew chuckled. "Yes, keep your shawl on. We'll go out to the mews directly."

As he led her through the other rooms and out the back door of the kitchen, Bridget looked about her carefully. She'd have to learn the lay of this place—and soon. Imagine prying Miss Linden's delight if she discovered that the new Marchioness of Haverly didn't know her way around her own home!

Bridget admired the stables. They were nicely kept,

clean and dry. The sweet smell of hay and the scent of horseflesh were perfume to her nostrils. She looked around anxiously. Where had they put the stallion? How did he like it in this strange new place?

But before she could accustom her eyes to the dimness and seek him out, Waterloo whiffled a greeting from a back stall. "There he is!" Heedless of her fine gown and flimsy satin slippers, she hurried back to him, quickly unlatching the door and throwing her arms around him. Dear Waterloo, he was safe. Laughing, she hugged his neck—she could count on him to always be her friend.

She trusted Andrew, but after all, he *was* a lord. And lords had peculiar ways of looking at things, peculiar ways of behaving.

Of course, Peter was a lord, too, but he was different—not so stern, not so—lordish. Laughing softly, she ran her hands over Waterloo's smooth coat. "Oh, you beautiful, beautiful horse! I missed you so much!"

" 'Ere now, miss!" A stableboy came hurrying up. "Ye shouldn't ought ta be in there with that 'orse. 'E's a stallion, 'e is. 'E might hurt ye."

Bridget turned. "Don't be silly. I raised this horse myself. He wouldn't hurt a soul."

The boy's eyes widened. "Begging yer pardon, miss, but he threw Jerry, 'ard, too."

"And what was this Jerry doing trying to ride *my* horse?" she demanded crossly. At home Papa had never let anyone else touch him. "Andrew!"

Andrew, who had hung back to see how Bridget dealt with the stable hands, now stepped forward. After this afternoon he should have known better than to worry. She could handle herself anywhere. "Yes?"

"Please, Andrew, give orders that no one is to ride Waterloo. No one but me."

He swallowed his smile. "I don't need to give such orders," he said. "You give them." He turned to the gaping stableboy. "Ned, this is Lady Haverly, my new wife. You'll obey her without question."

When the boy stilled, his mouth hanging open, Andrew went on. "The lady knows all there is to know about horses, so you needn't fear for her." Better for Ned to fear for himself, Andrew thought in amusement. If the boy didn't pay attention to Bridget, she'd no doubt blister his ears. He fastened Ned with a stern eye. "Do you understand?"

"Aye, milord," the boy said, the merest hint of a smile on his lips. "I understands. The lady gives orders. I obeys 'em."

Andrew nodded, turning to see Bridget actually smiling at the lad. "Then we shall get along well," she said. "Take good care of my stallion. I'll be out here often to see that you do."

The rest of the afternoon passed in uneventful fashion. Bridget spent some of it putting away her new clothes and unpacking her boxes from home.

She managed to get her breeches and boots out from under the books and hidden in a back corner of her closet before the maid Andrew insisted on sending her arrived. Peggy was a shy young girl, only lately gone into service, but trained as a lady's maid.

"Your other new gowns'll be here soon," Peggy said, hanging up the two dinner dresses they'd brought back with them from shopping and then moving to the forest green riding habit. "Ah, this, milady." She lifted a fold of the heavy velvet to her cheek. " 'Tis a lovely gown, it is. And just the color for you."

She stepped to the bed to fold the nightdresses and then put them away. " 'Tis grand of his Lordship to buy you so many nice things."

"Yes," Bridget agreed. Peggy seemed very interested in the clothes she was putting away. Did even servant girls dream of female fripperies? "I suppose it is." She glanced around the spacious room. "He's told me I can decorate this chamber however I please."

The maid's eyes widened. "Oh, milady. What great fun! Why, you can have some of them Chinese cupboards like the Regent has. All lacquered black and with them great dragons and such painted on them."

"Dragons?" Just in time, Bridget stopped herself from asking why any sensible person should *want* dragons in her bedroom. The Regent's Chinese taste must be the fashion just now. "I don't know," she said. "The room's not so bad. Maybe I'll just leave it as it is."

"Oh, milady!" Peggy's round face reddened with disappointment. Obviously *she* thought redecorating would be quite the thing. "But wouldn't that be hurting his Lordship's feelings, him being so nice to you and all?"

Bridget paused. She hadn't thought about that. The girl might have something there. Andrew had been very kind about all this. She certainly didn't want to offend him. "Perhaps you're right," she said. "I'll think about it. Maybe I will do it in another color."

Peggy clapped her hands in delight. "There's a shade of green, milady. A pretty green that'd go lovely with your reddish hair. I seen a lady wearing a gown of it just this

72

morning when I was out on an errand. And then you could put a touch of peach color here and there—to lighten things a bit. Oh, it'll be that beautiful, it will." She dropped her gaze shyly. "Just like you."

Bridget opened her mouth to reply that she was far from beautiful, but she closed it again without saying anything. Something about the girl reminded her of the country, she was so open and friendly. With a start of surprise, Bridget realized that she had never had a woman friend. Her only friends had been horses. "Thank you," she said. "Come, help me change for dinner, will you? Which of these two new gowns do you think is best?"

Chapter Eight

Andrew didn't go out again that afternoon, but anyway, it was too late for Bridget to slip into her riding clothes and take the stallion for a gallop through a city she barely knew. So she contented herself with thinking that the next morning her first order of business would be a good long ride. But that brought her to the question of where. Where could one really ride in this city with its thronged streets, its crowds of people all busy about their tasks?

She posed the question to Andrew at dinner where he had thoughtfully ordered their places set side by side instead of at opposite ends of the huge table. "Andrew, where do people around here go to ride?"

He paused, a forkful of roast duck halfway to his lips. "Well, we have several parks," he said. "But Hyde Park is where the *ton* usually goes to ride. Around five in the afternoon the crush there is as great as on the street."

She bit her lower lip in exasperation. She was liking this miserable city less and less; no one here seemed to behave with any sense. Though that was hardly Andrew's fault, still, a little of her irritation crept into her voice. "But if it's so crowded at that time, why does everyone go then? Why don't they go at some different hour?"

He looked at her thoughtfully while he finished chewing a mouthful of food. "Well, Bridget, it's rather like this. Lords and ladies don't ride to *ride* so much as they ride to be seen."

These people sounded more and more ridiculous. "Seen? But why should they want to be seen?"

He gave her a strange look. "The *ton* has odd ways, Bridget, I realize that. But I cannot explain them all to you. It would take far too long. So I suggest you just let me guide you in matters that have to do with this part of our life."

She frowned. Of course she would let him guide her in those matters. To do anything else in such a situation would be foolish. But now he was using that awful condescending tone, as though he knew everything and she knew nothing at all.

Well, she might not know much about being a lady— from the looks of it, this lady business was a silly muddle anyway—but she knew about horses. She knew more about horses than he did. She'd pit her knowledge in that area against his any day of the week—and she'd win, too.

And at least now she knew where she could go to ride. Maybe she'd take young Ned with her to the park. He looked like a bright boy. Maybe she'd put him in charge of Waterloo. The stallion would need companionship since she wouldn't be with him as much as she had been before. And it would be good for the boy, too, give him some standing in the stable. A servant's status depended to a great degree on the extent of his responsibilities, and being Waterloo's groom would gain Ned the respect of the others.

The evening passed slowly. Sitting in the library while she and Andrew read separate volumes, Bridget's thoughts strayed more than once to the fine new night-dress that Peggy would soon be laying out for her across the great bed. Would tonight be the night that Andrew would—

She stole a look at him over the top of her book. He looked very handsome, very grand, and for that reason, if perhaps for no other, very distant. Could he mean for theirs to be a marriage in name only? She should have asked Peggy about that—about how married lords and ladies comported themselves. And why they felt it neces-sary to sleep in separate beds. That seemed a foolish-ness—a waste of heat and of beds.

Mama's books had told her a lot, but there was so much she didn't know about society. Because of the books and the woman Papa had hired to teach her to read, she'd learned to speak the right way. At least, Andrew should have no complaint about that. But the stories in Mama's books, stories by men like Shakespeare, weren't about happy married people, but about people suffering from terrible human emotions like jealousy, rage, and revenge. There was nothing in those stories that could help her deal with Andrew. Nothing at all.

This sitting and saying nothing was definitely getting on her nerves. She put her book aside and looked at him directly. "Thank you for having Waterloo brought into the city for me. It's good to have him here with me. I missed him, though we were just separated for one day."

"I know you missed him. I know you're very fond of him." Andrew smiled at her. "He's your horse, of course, and he'll always remain your horse, but I would like to ride him some time. If that's agreeable with you."

She hesitated, unsure whether to tell him. "Yes, Andrew," she said, finally deciding he should know the truth, "that would be all right with me, but I feel I should warn you—Waterloo's a woman's horse."

Andrew put his book down and gave her a puzzled look. "Come now, Bridget, what do you mean? There's no such thing as a woman's horse. A horse is a horse. And that's all it is."

She might have known he'd take that attitude—men could be so stubborn sometimes—but she knew what she was talking about. Hadn't she raised the stallion herself from a tiny little foal? She sighed—that superior look on Andrew's face told her that there was nothing to be gained by arguing with him. Not a word she said would make any difference. He'd already made up his mind.

Still, she couldn't refrain from making one last comment. "I am only telling you what I know. He threw that Jerry, didn't he? At least, that's what Ned told us. You heard him."

Andrew's smile grew larger and more self-important. "Yes, but I suppose the lad Jerry wasn't much of a rider. At any rate, we'll see. I've never known a horse I couldn't ride."

Bridget swallowed her smile. Let him believe what he wanted to believe. He would anyway, no matter what she might say. But on Waterloo's back—or more accurately, flying off it—he would soon discover she was right.

In the meantime, she said, "Of course not. I know

you're an excellent rider. By the way, I was thinking of putting Ned in charge of Waterloo. Making the boy his personal groom. What do you think of my doing that?"

Andrew shrugged, his expression nonchalant. "Whatever you decide, Bridget. The stallion is yours."

That was one good thing. He didn't mean to interfere with Waterloo. "Fine," she said, giving him a grateful smile, "then that's what I'll do. I'll tell him tomorrow."

"Good." Andrew picked up his book again, and with a smothered sigh, she picked up her own. The evening stretched on before her, long and somehow lonely.

When the clock struck ten, Andrew shut his book and turned to Bridget. "Are you tired, my dear?"

"A little."

It was the first time he'd called her by a term of endearment, and somewhat to his surprise, he found it falling naturally from his lips. He decided to be direct. "Then I suggest you go on up and ring for Peggy. She can help you get ready for bed." He looked down at his book again. "And I'll be up a little later."

"Fine," Bridget said, getting to her feet. "That's what I'll do then."

Strange, Andrew thought, that he should find the situation rather embarrassing. She was the one without experience, not he. But he had not been accustomed to thinking of her as a female; indeed, he'd schooled himself *not* to think of her in that way. So this wrenching around of his perceptions might take some time. Still, he had always thought her beautiful, though no more beautiful in her new gown than she'd been in her leather breeches. The thought of those breeches sent the blood rushing to his face. He had wanted her then, too, though he'd denied it to himself. Well, now he didn't need to deny it.

He swallowed hastily, bringing his gaze back to her face. "That is, I'll be up if you don't mind." Some fine way to begin a marriage! He should simply have taken it for granted that she would expect him to come to her.

But then everything about this marriage was bewildering. He had never expected to win a wife in a horse race—actually, a wife *and* a stallion. And he had really no idea how to go about helping Bridget fit into what he was now perceiving was really a very constricted society.

Their chance meeting with the Lindens, though Bridget had handled it well, had made him aware, quite forcefully aware, that the *ton* would find his marriage subject for gossip and innuendo. And Bridget a topic of rare amusement.

He sighed. He didn't want her to be hurt, but he didn't quite know how to protect her. There were too many people like the Lindens out there, ready to talk about anyone, ready to make Bridget a laughingstock for things she didn't even understand.

She had reached the door and turned. The smile she sent him was shy, but definitely inviting. "I'll be waiting then, Andrew."

Smiling back, he watched her go, his beautiful young wife on her way to their wedding chamber. She was a wild thing, his Bridget, free and independent. Like the filly Sable, she wanted her own way, to follow her own path. With patience and loving care he had tamed Sable. But Bridget? He didn't know.

Chapter Nine

Early the next morning, in the big silk-draped bed, Bridget stirred, sighed briefly, and reached a hand out to the space beside her. But the space, though still warm, was empty. She stretched and opened her eyes. Andrew's getting up must have brought her from the depths of satisfying sleep. She looked toward the door to his room, but it was closed tight. Probably he had gone softly out, not wanting to wake her.

She stretched luxuriantly and smiled. The rising sun coming through the bed curtains set the golden coverlet to gleaming much like the precious metal itself. The whole chamber shimmered in a warm golden sheen, but nothing could be warmer, more golden, than the wonderful glowing feelings she had experienced in this very bed last night—in Andrew's arms.

She raised herself on one elbow. There on the floor lay her new blue nightdress, the one embroidered in dainty white roses. Probably she should get out of bed and pick it up. But she slid back under the warm covers, smiling.

The nightdress would still be there later. She was a lady now, and ladies could sleep late if they chose.

She turned on her side toward the place where Andrew had lain. The pillow still held the indentation of his head, and she fancied she could still smell the faint elusive masculine scent that was all his.

She laughed softly. At first last night Andrew had seemed embarrassed. That was odd because she knew for certain that she was not the only woman he'd bedded. That first day he'd come out to the stables, that day she'd heard the boys telling tales about him—one of the best men in the *ton,* they said, good with horses, and with beautiful young ladies fluttering about him like moths to a flame, and him burning them all.

She smiled to herself. If those young ladies had known the Andrew she'd known last night, they would have thrown themselves even more willingly into the fire. She sighed, her smile slowly disappearing. She liked Andrew, she liked being his wife. And what they'd done last night—well, Papa had been quite right. She liked that, too, she liked it quite a lot.

But still, it didn't seem right—Papa tricking Andrew about the wager. She'd tried to tell him she was sorry about it, but he'd hushed her with a kiss—that was after her nightdress hit the floor—and said to never mind, he was sure they'd deal quite well together. And then he'd shown her *how* they would deal.

Their lovemaking was much better, actually, than the way the horses did it. Not nearly as quick or as violent. And for the first time in her life she felt sorry for a horse— who couldn't possibly know those wonderful, golden, shimmering waves of warmth that spread over her entire body.

Finally she pushed back the silken covers. It was late to be lying abed—late for her, anyway. There were things she meant to do today: to speak to Ned about caring for Waterloo, to go for her long-awaited ride on the stallion, to send Peggy for yard-good samples so they could begin to think about redecorating the room. And she hoped that she and Andrew could ride out to see Papa to tell him the stables were safe. And he, too.

She washed and dressed, not even thinking till she was almost finished that she should have rung the bell for Peggy. Well, time enough to start being a lady tomorrow. She ran the brush through her hair and went downstairs.

The breakfast room was empty except for the patiently waiting footman. "His Lordship?" she asked. "Has he gone out?"

The footman nodded. "Yes, my Lady, but I heard him tell Mr. Purvey he'd be back directly."

"Thank you." Bridget picked up a plate and surveyed the sideboard. She really must ask Andrew the reason for so much food.

At that moment Andrew was outside White's, engaged in conversation with Peter, who had run into him as they approached the club's sacred precincts. "My word," Peter exclaimed, showing his teeth in a devilish grin. "If it isn't the man all London's talking about! Shall we go in and have a glass together?"

"Yes," Andrew said. "From the sound of things, I shall need it."

Peter's grin grew even bigger. "You mean you aren't finding married life to your liking?"

Thinking of last night, Andrew experienced a surge of warmth. "Married life is—so far at least—quite to my liking. This is something else."

"How do you suppose the news got about so quickly?" Peter asked as they found a table. "Why, six or eight people must have informed me already this morning."

Andrew dropped into a chair, glowering. "It's those abominable Lindens! Too bad they can't be shrunk and put on display at Farrington's Folly like Lady Elizabeth's shrunken heads."

"A charming idea," Peter agreed, summoning a waiter. "But one I'm afraid will never achieve the Lindens' assent. Besides, can you imagine the monumental task of shrinking Lady Linden?" He paused to order, remaining silent till the waiter left. Then he said, "I take it you ran into the messengers of scandal sometime yesterday."

Andrew nodded. "Yes, I did. On Bond Street. And that miserable slip of a daughter shrilled out that Bridget was Durabian's daughter. All heads turned, you can believe, to see what all the yapping was about."

Peter shrugged. "I don't see how you could expect to keep it a secret. Either your marriage or Bridget's parentage." He grinned. "I mean, Bridget's no ordinary wife. She won't be a sit-at-home."

"Don't I know it," Andrew agreed with a half groan. "But how can I take her out in company? Why, yesterday she was outraged to find that we use different spoons for the soup, said it was a waste."

He found himself growing red and lowered his voice. "And do you know what else she told me?"

Peter looked agreeably curious. "No, what?"

Andrew leaned closer. "That she couldn't understand why wealthy people are so foolish."

Peter grinned. "We are, I suppose, at least to her, but did she mention specifics?"

Andrew nodded. "Oh, yes, she said it was a waste for married people to sleep apart—a waste of space, of beds, and of—" He paused, unaccountably embarrassed. "And of warm bodies."

Peter's guffaw echoed through the dining room, causing several grizzled heads to turn questioningly in their direction. He smiled at them. "That's Bridget," he said, lowering his voice. "You've got quite a filly there, Andrew, my boy. Are you going to be able to tame her?"

Remembering last night, Andrew smiled. "There's never been a filly I couldn't tame. I don't expect Bridget to be any different." He hesitated. "But don't you dare tell her I said so!"

Bridget enjoyed the ride out to the stables. Fortunately Andrew had assumed she'd ride the stallion and he the filly, so there was no problem there. The day was sunny, Andrew was a pleasant companion, and riding Waterloo was, as always, exhilarating.

But the new riding habit was a nuisance, always tangling about her legs in the most infuriating fashion. It must have been men who put women in skirts, she thought with some annoyance. No one else could have come up with such a cumbersome way of dressing.

The sidesaddle, too, though a good one and as comfortable as such a saddle could be, was aggravatingly constricting. Surely no man had ever attempted to ride in such a ridiculous seat.

But she had not suggested to Andrew that she wear her breeches and ride astride. She had a strong feeling that he would not find such attire appropriate, and since she didn't wish to directly go against his wishes, it would be better if she didn't know what those wishes were.

She would save her breeches for when she was alone. She and Ned had had quite a satisfactory talk. He had agreed—quite happily—to serve as the stallion's personal groom and to show her about the city.

As they neared the stables, she felt an unaccountable shyness. What should she say to Papa today? Should she tell him that she knew about his debts and that Andrew had paid them for him? She frowned. Papa was such a proud man. It must embarrass him terribly to be beholden to his daughter's husband. Maybe she should just be quiet about it and preserve his pride.

As they rode into the yard, Papa came out of the tack room. "Papa!" she called, pulling up the stallion so sharply that he tossed his head and snorted, throwing her an injured look over his shoulder.

"Sorry, boy," she said, stroking his smooth neck. "I'll be more careful. I promise."

She managed to slide down from the horse before Andrew could get to her. In spite of last night, she didn't appreciate needing a mans's help, help she wouldn't need at all if she hadn't been forced to wear these stupid female clothes.

She straightened the skirt, took a step toward Papa, caught a toe in her hem, and catapulted right into Andrew's arms. He caught her easily and set her back on her feet.

"Careful, love," he said softly, smiling down at her. For a moment she remembered the night before and her knees went all wobbly, so wobbly she had to cling to his arms for support.

But the moment passed and she turned. "Papa, how are you?"

A frown crossed his face and was instantly gone. "And how should I be?" he asked, his voice hearty. "I'm as well as ever I've been. And things here are fine," he went on. "We've a new foal in the south paddock. Born yester eve, it was. A pretty little thing."

So he wasn't going to say anything about his debts.

He looked her over carefully. "Ye're looking quite the lady, Bridget. 'Tis pleased I am to be seeing ye looking so well."

She felt that shyness again and murmured, "Thank you, Papa."

He grinned at her. "Well, girl, aren't ye going to have a look at the new foal? I swear, that mare kept looking round the whole of the time. Like as if she wondered why ye weren't there."

"Of course, Papa. I'll go right now." She lifted the heavy skirt and set off across the grass. Men were so comical. If Papa wanted to talk to Andrew alone, maybe to thank him for paying his IOUs, why didn't he just say he wanted to talk to him? Why go through all this silliness and pretending? But she would like to see the foal. Baby horses were always beautiful.

* * *

Andrew watched as Bridget, clutching the unaccustomed weight of her habit skirt, made her way toward the paddock. For a moment he wished her back in her breeches again. He was going to miss those pants.

"Well now, milord," Durabian said, clearing his throat and pulling his pipe from one pocket and his tobacco pouch from the other. "Yer factor come here yesterday and he told me what ye done. It weren't necessary, milord. That is, I was ready to go to prison." He swallowed, tamping tobacco into the bowl of the pipe. "Bridget and her horse was safe with ye. That were me only concern." He reddened. "I never meant that ye should—"

Andrew nodded. "I think I understand. But after I discovered your problem, I wished to correct it."

Durabian cleared his throat again, lit the pipe, puffing heavily. "And I thank ye fer it, but—"

"No buts," Andrew replied. "I couldn't let Wichersham have your stables, now could I?"

Durabian managed a grim smile. "No, milord. He's a mean 'un, Wichersham is. Mean as ever they come." He hesitated. "Bridget, does she be knowing 'bout all this?"

Andrew swallowed. Should he tell? But he owed the man the truth. "She knows about the gambling debts," he said.

Durabian's face fell. "I was hoping that—"

"But she doesn't know the name of the man who held your notes." Andrew shook his head. "Wichersham? Really, man. How could you even wager with the likes of him?"

"I didn't, milord." Durabian looked pained. "Me wagers was with others. Wichersham, he bought up me vowels. I was that surprised, I was."

Andrew considered Durabian's averted eyes. There was more to this than that. The man was hiding something. Should he push to find out what it was?

But he had to think about Bridget—and her feelings. She obviously adored her father. If he pushed to find out the rest of this thing, and Bridget asked him about it—what would he do then? It was bound to be something unfortunate, and it was obviously something her father wanted to keep from her.

Andrew swallowed a sigh. He could well understand that. He wanted to protect her himself. Bridget did that to a man. He'd never know a woman like her. So innocent and yet abandoned. Naive and trusting. Trusting *him*.

He turned to her father. "Durabian, I'll ask you this once—and once only."

Durabian turned from watching Bridget pick her way across the grass. "Aye, milord, what—"

"Please, you're my wife's father. Call me Andrew."

A strange look crossed the man's face. "I'll do that— Andrew. If yer sure 'tis what ye want."

That was one of the few things he *was* sure of. "I'm sure."

"Then Andrew it is." Durabian almost smiled. "But I doubt ye'll be calling me Da now. 'Tis a little much, that."

Andrew smiled, too. How could he help not smiling at such a possibility? "Yes, I suppose it is. But now for my question."

For a minute he thought the man would look away again, but Durabian's gaze held steady. "Ask it then."

Andrew hesitated, wondering how best to put the query. "I am Bridget's husband now. And I mean to take good care of her. We paid the notes Wichersham held. So you're safe enough there. But is there anything else I need to know, anything that might be harmful to Bridget?"

Durabian heaved a great sigh, blowing out a cloud of fragrant smoke. "No, Andrew. As yer wife, Bridget is safe. That's all I need—fer her to be safe."

Andrew thought about this. There was still something else, something Durabian didn't want him to know. But if the man said Bridget was safe, then she was safe. And, Andrew decided, he would leave it at that. "Very well," he said. "I just wanted to know."

Chapter Ten

The next morning the sun woke Bridget. She turned carefully, but Andrew had left her bed. Perhaps he'd gone back to his own chamber in the night. Or perhaps he had already gone off about estate business. He was, after all, a man of great responsibilities.

She glanced at the clock. No, it was too early for most lords to be up and about. If she'd learned one thing in her few days as a lady, it was that quality slept late, very late.

With a grin she slid out from under the covers and hurried to her closet. She meant to use that lateness to her advantage.

Minutes later she was in her breeches and out in the stables. Ned, good boy, was ready. So was Waterloo. More than ready, he pulled eagerly at the bridle, neighing happily when he heard her approaching.

Ned's eyes widened when he saw what she was wearing. He even opened his mouth but closed it again without saying anything. His eyes nearly bugged out of his head when she quickly unbuckled Waterloo's sidesaddle and replaced it with one of Andrew's own.

She saw he had saddled another animal for himself. "Good," she said briskly, cramming her hair up under her cap. "We'll be off then."

Despite the early hour, the streets were not deserted. Lords and ladies might be still abed, but the little people, those who had to earn their daily bread, were already hard at work. Shopgirls wielded their brooms industriously at doorsteps, delivery boys hurried by with packages, a chimney sweep herded his blackened helpers down the street ahead of him. And in a sheltered doorway, two little girls piled wildflowers in shabby baskets.

Bridget heaved a sigh. The city was a bad place to be poor. In the country the poor at least had a chance to raise some food. Here they had to scrabble for every bite. Here they had no green grass, no space, and very little sun.

For a while her sadness weighed down on her like a heavy blanket, but eventually the beauty of the park raised her spirits. Such a vast expanse of green—none of it needed for crops or pasture—was something she'd never seen before. From a grove of trees several deer stared at her, not at all frightened.

"They're so tame," she murmured to the boy.

"Pertected," Ned said. "Them's the King's deer."

Bridget nodded, but she didn't want to think of deer or kings or anything except the restive stallion between her knees. He wanted to run—and so did she.

"You needn't try to keep up with us," she told Ned. "You won't be able to, anyhow."

The boy grinned. "I knows that, milady. That 'un, 'e goes like the wind, 'e do."

Bridget nodded. "Just wait for us." When she chirruped, Waterloo took off in a great eager leap, almost immediately hitting a full gallop. She leaned into the wind, savoring its rush over her face, exulting in the raw power of the great beast beneath her. In some strange way they were one—one creature of power and grace. One creature faster than the wind itself.

This was what she'd always lived for—at least as far back as she could remember. To ride. It had always seemed to her the most glorious experience in the world—to ride with utter abandon at the fastest gallop, horse and rider as one. But that was before she and Andrew had—

Feeling her face heat up, she swallowed hastily. Marriage was all right. Well, it was more than all right, much more. But she would always love to ride, to gallop into the wind, to feel the world rushing by.

She gave the stallion his head, letting him run off some of his high spirits. And eventually, when he slowed, she turned him back the way they'd come. Ned was just a dot in the far distance, waiting patiently. She headed Waterloo toward him.

The warm sun felt good on her upturned face. She pulled off her cap, letting her hair fall free. That was what she'd done that first day she'd met Andrew, pulled off her cap to let him know that it wasn't a stableboy he was clapping so familiarly on the shoulder. Then she'd tried to freeze him with her frostiest look. But after he'd apologized, she couldn't stay angry with him.

She smiled. And now she was Andrew's wife. How strange life could be.

Ned looked around a trifle anxiously. "Milady, it be

getting on into morning. Quality, it'll be stirring soon. And 'is Lordship—"

The boy ground to a halt, then stammered on. "I know 'e ain't said not to—leastways not as *I* know of. But mayhap we should be getting back."

Bridget nodded. "You're right, Ned. He hasn't said not to ride in the morning like this." She gave the boy a warm smile. "But I don't think we need to tell him about it. At least not yet. We'll keep it our secret. All right?"

The boy's face shone with loyalty, but his eyes betrayed misgiving. "Aye, milady. 'E did tell me ye was to be obeyed."

"Yes, he did." She really shouldn't be asking the boy to keep secrets for her. If Andrew found out and was angered, Ned could lose his place.

She leaned forward to stroke Waterloo's great neck. As always, touching him was a comfort. It wasn't likely that Andrew would be so cruel as to send the boy packing, but if Ned did lose his place, she could send him to Papa. Papa could always use another boy who was handy with horses.

The thought of Papa made her frown. Andrew had been very good to Papa, getting him out of that awful gambling mess. Maybe she *should* ask Andrew about early morning rides. But really, what harm did they do? Waterloo got his run. She got hers. And no one saw them. Surely there was no harm in that.

She stuffed her hair back up under her cap and gave the horse a pat. "Come on, Ned. Time to go home."

Bridget made it through the kitchen and up the back stairs to her room without seeing any servants. The understaff wouldn't report her comings and goings to her husband, but she rather felt that the stiff butler Purvey might feel duty bound to tell if he saw his mistress sneaking up the back stairs in shabby leather breeches. Mrs. Purvey might just keep silent.

She closed her door, rang for Peggy, and stripped off her riding clothes. It was too bad ladies led such restricted lives. She threw her breeches and other things into the back corner of the closet and turned to the basin to wash. Maybe later, after she and Andrew had been married a little longer, she could explain it to him, get him to see how foolish ladies clothing really was.

The door opened. "There you are, milady. His Lordship was asking after you."

"I went for a ride," Bridget said, turning away so Peggy couldn't see the flush rising to her cheeks. "I took a groom along, of course."

Peggy nodded, crossing to the closet for a gown. "The rest of your new things ought to be coming soon. I'm betting they'll be that lovely." She frowned. "Why, you've hung up your habit yourself. And just like I left it." She shook her head. "You shouldn't be doing my work, milady. It ain't decent, it ain't."

"I won't do it again," Bridget said quickly. Next time she'd remember to drop the habit on the floor. There was no need to involve Peggy in this business.

Her ride kept Bridget in good spirits till midafternoon, but by then she had been over the whole house—huge place that it was—and had every hall and passageway firmly fixed in her mind.

She'd also had long talks about the running of the household with Cook and Mrs. Purvey, talks that had been somewhat confusing to everyone, since *they* seemed to be expecting orders from *her*. And when she said, "Everything looks fine, go on as usual," they'd both looked surprised.

Changing things around must be something ladies liked to do. She herself could see no purpose in changing something just for the sake of showing she could. If things were running smoothly, they should be left alone to go on the same way. That made sense.

Now she was seated in the sitting room, glaring at the piece of unfortunate needlepoint she held in her hands. Why hadn't she just read a book?

Needlepoint was a complete mystery to her. Another useless thing that ladies did. They seemed a fairly useless lot all round, these ladies. But perhaps it wasn't entirely their fault.

Look at the idiotic clothes they had to wear. Even walking was something she had to pay attention to. She couldn't just go striding along like she had in her breeches.

With a sigh she dropped the needlework into its basket. Mrs. Purvey had been the soul of patience, sending a maid out for the sampler and yarn and showing over and over how each stitch should be done.

And Bridget had tried. But the yarn was always tangling and knotting. Her stitches were lumpy and uneven. And the design—insipid flowers arranged in an equally insipid vase—was dull, dull, dull. Now if there had been horses in it, the design might have been worth a pricked finger or two. She might even have stuck with it to the end.

She got up and began to pace the hearth rug. She

missed the horses and the stables. Papa, too, of course. But most of all the horses. They made far better friends than people.

She turned toward the door. Maybe she'd just grab her shawl and step out for a visit with Waterloo. She should get acquainted with Andrew's horses, too. There hadn't been time for that yet.

But she had only taken one step when Purvey appeared in the doorway. "Lady Linden and Miss Martine Linden," he intoned.

Bridget stopped in her tracks. Not those two! Now what should she do? "Andr—Lord Haverly isn't at home."

Purvey gave her a strange look, so fleeting she could recognize nothing but that it was odd. "The ladies have come to call on you, milady."

"Oh dear!" she cried. "What do I do now?" It was then she recognized the emotion on Purvey's face. It was surprise.

He cleared his throat. "It is customary," he said, "to receive lady callers in here or in the morning room. And to serve tea." He hesitated. "Your Ladyship *could* have me say you're not at home."

The prospect was tempting, but she was not a liar. And besides, it seemed cowardly. "No, Purvey. Bring them in and serve the tea."

He started toward the door.

"Wait!" She smoothed her skirt. "Do I look all right?"

For a moment it appeared he might actually smile, but he only nodded and said, "You look fine, milady. Very well."

She pushed the offending needlework down out of sight and settled herself in her chair. Now above all she must guard her speech. The Lindens would repeat every word she said—and no doubt some she didn't.

"My dear Lady Haverly!" Lady Linden swept into the room like a walking carnival tent, the resemblance heightened by the fact that her gown was bright orange, striped in bilious green. Her massive arms jangled with bracelets and her pudgy fingers glittered with rings. And from beneath an enormous bonnet that looked very much like a huge cabbage split endways, the lady's beady little eyes took in every feature of Bridget's dress and person.

Dear God, Bridget thought, what a good thing she was no longer wearing her breeches. "Won't you sit down?" she invited politely.

Lady Linden nodded. Her stickish daughter, trailing behind her in a gown and bonnet as drab as her mother's were vivid, declined a chair and commenced pacing round the room in a most annoying manner, peering at paintings and examining vases as though she meant to purchase the lot.

Lady Linden settled her ponderous bulk into a chair. When it creaked in protest but didn't collapse, Bridget breathed a sigh of relief. For a moment there she hadn't been sure.

"Well now," said Lady Linden, fixing her gaze on Bridget's face, "aren't you the lucky one?"

"I beg your pardon?"

Lady Linden glanced around, taking in the room's rich furnishings. "Marrying all this. Tell me, my dear, how *did* you manage it?"

Why, the old battle ax was even worse than Andrew had painted her! But remembering his warning, Bridget smiled sweetly. "I'm afraid I can't help you there, Lady

Linden. Our marriage was arranged in the traditional fashion by my pa—by my father."

Lady Linden's eyes glittered with curiosity. "Indeed, and did he tell you why?"

Bridget felt her hackles rising. This woman was impossibly rude. But Andrew had been very stern about this—she must not lose her temper, he said, no matter what the provocation. She forced her lips into another false smile. "I suppose my father wanted me to marry a man he liked. He and Andrew are great friends."

That much was true, at least. She made herself sit still, kept herself from looking toward the door. Why didn't Andrew come home?

For some moments Lady Linden seemed lost in thought. Then she chuckled, the folds of flesh under her chin shivering in a fascinating rhythm. "What a novel way of looking at things, my dear." She patted her curls. "Of course it was his Lordship's money—and the title, you know—that made your father feel so friendly toward him."

Feeling her hands curl into fists, Bridget buried them in her skirts, The old busybody had no right to talk about Papa like that! She'd tell her a thing or two. Maybe rearrange those false curls and put a few holes in that enormous—

But wait! She couldn't do that. She couldn't embarrass Andrew by behaving like a shrewish fishwife, brawling with guests in their home.

"My father and my husband," she said, keeping her voice even, "are both great lovers of horses. That was what first brought them together."

"And you," Lady Linden said pointedly. "I understand *you* train horses."

"I have," Bridget said. Let the old witch make something of that! "Horses are—"

"Such nasty creatures," Miss Linden interjected with great venom. "Always stepping on one's feet." Her thin nose quivered in indignation. "I suppose they're all right for pulling carriages and such." She elevated her nose another inch. "But that one should want to *work* with them! Be around them constantly. Ugh! A lady couldn't possibly do that!"

For a moment Bridget's heart fell, but then she forced herself to smile again. Andrew wouldn't keep her from the horses—he'd promised. "I'm afraid you're wrong," she said. "A lady *can* work with horses. And I intend to do just that."

Lady Linden's chuckle took her by surprise. What did the old shrew find so amusing now?

"Oh my dear, how droll. I see now why they've given you that adorable nickname."

"What nickname?"

"You mean you haven't heard?" Lady Linden's little eyes gleamed with evident enjoyment, and her pudgy fingers teased a false curl that dangled from under the cabbage hat. "Why, they're saying *you're* his Lordship's newest filly. And they're recording bets at White's."

"Bets?" Bridget mumbled, fighting to keep her hands off the fat neck of this infuriating creature.

"Of course," Lady Linden went on. "You know how these men are—" She paused to wave a pudgy hand dramatically. "Well, perhaps you don't know. But men bet constantly on anything. That's why White's keeps the betting book—to record their bets. So there'll be no mistakes."

"And what," Bridget asked through lips gone wooden, "are they betting about us?"

Lady Linden's laughter shivered the hair on the back of Bridget's neck and set her teeth on edge.

"Why, my dear," the lady said with great gusto, "they say the odds are in his Lordship's favor. And they're betting he will tame *you.*"

Chapter Eleven

The surge of outraged anger that swept through Bridget almost lifted her right off her chair, but with Lady Linden's sharp eyes on her she kept herself under control. "How droll!" she repeated gaily, hoping that only she could hear the emptiness of her laughter. "How extremely droll."

She didn't quite know how she did it, but she managed to be civil to the old battle ax, and even to her prowling daughter, though it grew harder and harder. To listen— or pretend to listen—to Lady's Linden newest store of *on-dits*. Even to now and then make some reply to her. And finally, mercifully, the two made their exaggerated goodbyes and departed in a flurry of Lady Linden's brilliant orange skirts.

Bridget waited only till the front door closed solidly behind them. Then she grabbed her shawl and, muttering curses that would have shocked even Papa, hurried out to the stable.

When she opened the door and stepped in, the warm sweet fragrance of horseflesh and hay enveloped her. As always, it was like coming home. She pulled in a deep breath and just stood there, letting the familiar sounds and smells soothe her senses and calm her anger.

A welcoming whicker from the interior of the stable told her Waterloo had scented her presence. "I'm coming," she called. She'd have to talk to Ned about some place to go riding in the afternoons. If she had to endure many visitors like the Lindens, she'd be needing the release of a good gallop more than once a day.

That Lady Linden! Imagine her repeating a thing like that. So they were betting on Andrew taming his new wife. She'd see about that!

When Andrew's carriage turned the corner approaching home, he saw another pulling away—the Lindens' carriage. He called softly up to his driver. "Slow down, James."

As the carriages passed, he got a glimpse of bright orange. But he turned almost instantly, shielding his face from the view of those passing. Thank goodness he hadn't arrived home any sooner. At the moment another visit with the Lindens was more than he could stand.

It was bad enough that all London was talking about him—about him and Bridget, and their unusual liaison. But to have the Lindens running about spreading their invidious half-lies—that was the outside of enough. He only hoped that Bridget had managed to endure their visit without too much distress. The Lindens could be offensive, as he knew only too well—and Bridget had an Irish temper.

Suddenly concerned, he hurried into the house. "Her Ladyship?" he asked the butler. "Where is she?"

"I believe her Ladyship has gone out to the stable," Purvey said soberly.

Andrew nodded. "To see her horse, no doubt."

Purvey looked even stiffer than usual. "Yes, milord. I believe so. She had some visitors earlier—Lady Linden and her daughter."

Andrew frowned. "A bothersome pair. I saw them leaving."

"Yes, milord." Purvey hesitated. "I offered to say her Ladyship was not at home, but she said she would see the visitors. If I might add, milord, she seemed to think that being 'not at home' was somehow—wrong."

Andrew smiled. "Thank you, Purvey. I'm afraid she's a little raw yet. I'll have to inform her of the niceties of receiving visitors."

Purvey nodded solemnly. "That's true, milord, but still she does have a way about her."

Andrew headed immediately for the stable. He had to tell Bridget about Lady Conyngham's upcoming soiree. He sighed. He wasn't at all sure Bridget was ready to go out in society, but since he hadn't been quick enough with his excuses, they were committed to attend the function. Besides, they might as well get it over with. They had to appear at something before long. Otherwise people would talk. He sighed again. There would be talk no matter what.

He found Bridget where he had expected, at Waterloo's stall, murmuring sweet nothings to the stallion. For a moment he felt a twinge of something very like envy. Ridiculous, he told himself with an inner smile—how could he be envious of a horse!

"Hello, my dear." He joined her in the box stall, sliding

an arm around her slender waist. "I have good news for you. We've been invited to a soiree Wednesday next."

She turned, her expression full of hesitation. "Hello, Andrew. What kind of soiree?"

He shrugged. "Just the usual thing. Many people, much food. And no doubt a great deal of empty talk."

She wrinkled her nose. "Talk! I don't want to go. I've had enough *talk* to last me a long time."

He sighed. From the sound of it, Bridget wasn't in a good mood. "I'm sure, my dear. But I'm afraid I've already accepted Lady Conyngham's invitation." He smiled. "You can wear one of your new gowns."

She gave him a bitter look. "Andrew! I don't want to go."

He squeezed her waist. "Bridget, we've got to go about in society. After all, I want to show off my beautiful wife."

He bent to kiss her soft neck. "You're just a little upset today, that's all. I saw the Lindens' carriage leaving. How was your visit?"

She turned toward him, her lovely face flushed with anger. "Oh Andrew, I don't know how you can even bear to speak to them. The Lindens are the meanest, most despicable creatures alive."

An unnerving suspicion hit him. "Bridget, they didn't—You didn't—You didn't let them—"

She frowned. "I didn't let them provoke me, no. Oh, I was the perfect lady, whatever *that* is. But that woman, that awful, awful creature! Something should be done about her."

He tried a little humor. "The other day I suggested to Peter that she be shrunk and put on display with Lady

Elizabeth's shrunken heads." He chuckled. "An admirable idea, but unfortunately not feasible."

Bridget didn't laugh. "She told me the most horrible things," she said, her voice taut with anger. "The most horrible things about people I've never even heard of."

She gave him an even angrier look. "And before that she told me something else—something really disgusting."

He wracked his brain. Disgusting? What could the fat old tattletale have known that would make Bridget so angry? "You mustn't pay any attention to her." He drew Bridget into the circle of his arm again. "Lady Linden will do anything, say anything, to get another *on-dit* to carry about town."

Bridget felt so tense in his arms, angry and withdrawn. She didn't lean against him or turn her face to his for a kiss. She just stood there—stiff and wooden. He felt a spreading sense of discomfort, of loss. It was true that he'd married her because of the wager, but he cared about her. He really cared about her.

Giving in to the inevitable, he asked, "What did Lady Linden say to you?"

Bridget eased out of his grasp, moving away and leaning against the horse instead. He felt that twinge of envy again. "She said—she said they were calling me your *filly*. Betting on us. And then she said that the odds were in your favor. That people bet you would *tame* me."

He heard the anger, the sheer outrage, in her taut voice. He didn't like her being talked about. He didn't like it for himself either. But he couldn't prevent it. He moved toward her, put a placating hand on her shoulder. "Little do they know," he whispered, pitching his voice low and leaning toward her ear. "Little do they know that it's *you* who have tamed *me*."

He felt the tension slowly leaving her body, her flesh literally unstiffening beneath his fingers.

"Bridget, love," he whispered, his voice gone hoarse with very real desire. "You know you have me in your pocket. What do we care what people say?"

She turned to him, raising her face to his. "You're right, Andrew," she said. "We don't care. We don't care at all." And she put her arms around his neck, pulled his head down, and kissed him. Kissed him quite thoroughly—and without any regard for the stableboys.

The next morning Bridget slipped out for her ride with a lighter heart. Hadn't Andrew said he didn't care what people said? That meant he wouldn't mind about her early morning rides. Still, she saw no real reason to tell him.

This morning her gallop was even more invigorating than usual. She felt so good—so alive. The greens of the park and the bright blue of the sky seemed so vibrant and her body even more in tune with the stallion's than usual.

Life, she thought as they headed the horses back through the crowded streets toward the great house, life was very good. Papa was safe. She had Waterloo. And being married to Andrew was better, much better, than she could ever have imagined.

"Flowers?" a thin voice piped. "Buy me wild flowers? Picked fresh this morning."

Bridget looked down. A waif stood there—a little girl in dirty gray rags, her greasy blond hair straggling down around her pale pinched face. Just a slip of a thing. And so young.

Waterloo reached out, nipping a mouthful of flowers from the proffered nosegay. " 'Ere now!" the waif cried. "You stop it. You can't have me flowers less'n the lady buys 'em first."

Bridget smiled. The child was small, but she faced up without fear to the great stallion.

"Yer a pretty 'orse," she said. "But I gots to eat, too. And flowers won't do fer me."

She held up the now-lopsided nosegay. "Flowers, milady? Fresh-picked flowers."

Bridget reached in her pocket, then realized she'd brought no coins with her. "I've no money with me today," she said. "But I'll have some tomorrow."

She saw hope leaving the child's eyes. "I pass here every morning," she went on.

The child nodded. "I seen you." She reached out a dirty hand and stroked the great horse's nose. "Seen 'im, too."

"Yes," Bridget said. "Now, I'll have a nosegay from you every day. Maybe two. If you're here when I pass."

The child smiled then. "Oh, I'll be 'ere, milady. This 'ere's me corner. I'm 'ere ever day." She stepped aside. "And thank 'ee."

Bridget clicked to the stallion and he headed on homeward, Ned trailing behind. She tried to think of other things, but the child's face had looked so pinched. She was hungry, poor thing, and maybe even cold.

By the time they'd reached home, Bridget had made up her mind. She swung down from the stallion and turned to the boy. "Take care of him," she told Ned. "But don't unsaddle your horse. I'm going into the house to get some coins. I want you to take them back to that little girl." She had an awful thought. "You can find her again, can't you?"

Ned nodded. "Aye, milady, I 'members the corner."

She started toward the door. "I'll get several coins." Thank goodness Papa had always been generous with her. She had a small store of money put away. "She looked so hungry."

"Yer Ladyship," Ned said, his voice gone strained.

Bridget turned. "Yes?"

" 'Er da—or whatever 'e is—'e'll take money. Prob'ly spend it on blue ruin—gin. Be better to send 'er a bun or a bit a meat extra. I can tell 'er to eat it while she's selling."

"Of course, Ned! That's the way to do it." Bridget gave him a big smile. "I'll have Cook fix something. And I'll get the coins." She clapped him on the shoulder. "You're a good boy, Ned, a really good boy. I'm lucky you're here."

The boy's face went crimson and he turned away mumbling, "I'd best take care a the stallion now."

When Ned returned an hour later, Bridget had washed and changed into her day gown, and gone back to the stable to wait with Waterloo. The familiar smells and sounds gave her comfort that no place else could. It had always been that way. As a tiny little girl she'd found the stable her favorite hiding place.

A noise by the door made her look up. Thank goodness, the waiting was over. "Did you find her?" she asked anxiously.

Ned grinned, twisting his cap between his hands. "Aye, milady, that I did. She were on 'er corner, just like she said. She give me these two—prettiest nosegays she 'ad." He held them out.

Bridget raised them to her nose and sniffed. "They smell wonderful. Tell me everything that happened."

Ned nodded. "Well, yer Ladyship, when she saw that great chunk a meat and bread, why, she most cried. She were that grateful."

"But did she eat it?" Bridget asked anxiously. "I wanted *her* to have it."

"She broke it in 'alf," Ned said, using his hands to mimic the action. "And when I asked 'er why, she said she was keeping 'alf fer 'er little sister what's working the next corner." He looked a little anxious. "So, knowing 'ow worrid ye was, why, I took it to 'er sister. That's what took me so long."

"Good! That's good. Did you find out about their parents?" Bridget asked impatiently. "Where do they live?"

Ned frowned and looked down. "Gone, yer Ladyship. Dead and gone."

"Oh no! Then who—"

"The bigger one, name of Elsie, she told me after their folks died the neighbors took 'em in. They all sells the flowers, but the old man, 'e drinks the money right up."

Bridget straightened. "We'll take some meat and some bread to her every day. We'll see to it."

Ned's usual smile returned. "She'll be that happy," he said. He looked awkwardly down at his feet. "I—I best get to work."

Bridget nodded. "Yes, Ned, and thank you again for doing this for me."

"Tweren't nothing," Ned said soberly. "Me ma—bless 'er kind soul—she always said 'twas good to be 'elping folks. And she were right."

Chapter Twelve

Lord and Lady Conyngham's mansion blazed with light. In front of its great door, carriage after carriage paused to disgorge richly appareled occupants. When they finally reached the entrance, Andrew helped Bridget descend from the carriage and took her arm to lead her to the great stairs.

Bridget looked around with an exclamation of dismay. "Andrew, why didn't you tell me it would be like this? All these people!"

He shrugged. Sometimes her naiveté was amusing. But sometimes it was not. This was just another soiree—nothing special, nothing special at all. "There are always a lot of people attending something like this. But you needn't worry. They're just people!"

That wasn't entirely correct. He had believed it once, when he was young and carefree—that gossip meant nothing to him. And actually then it hadn't. But after Tom's death, after the title fell on *his* shoulders, Andrew had realized what damage wagging tongues could actually do. His mother had suffered a great deal from the venomous attacks of those who thought themselves her betters, but she had been shy, delicate, a tender flower, without Bridget's practical approach to life, without her ability to fight back.

And there was another thing that made Bridget different from the ladies of the *ton*. She had quite a lot of zest for life. He couldn't imagine the lively, vibrant Bridget ever complaining about ennui like so many ladies of his acquaintance. But then, her existence wasn't encompassed by drawing rooms and sitting rooms, by petty call-making and ridiculous small talk, by the effort to become the belle of the ball. He could not imagine Bridget spending hours on her appearance. She would find that kind of thing a bothersome waste of time.

But in spite of the ease—and speed—with which she'd dressed this evening, Bridget was looking her most beautiful. Her gown of deep green sarcenet was gathered under the bosom with narrow ribbons of white velvet. From there the gown flowed straight to the floor where it met her matching satin slippers. The gown's long narrow sleeves were also trimmed with narrow white velvet, its square neck edged with it. Her lovely auburn hair, which had been curled into tight ringlets and piled on the top of her head, was tied with more white ribbon.

Among the cream of London's bejeweled and richly clad ladies, Bridget stood out. She was a diamond of the first water, his Bridget.

At the top of the stairs, he drew her arm through his and led her toward the receiving line. Ever the proper hostess, Lady Conyngham smiled beatifically. "Lady Haverly, we've heard so much about you. So pleased to make your acquaintance."

"Thank you," Bridget said, ignoring the first comment. "It was kind of you to invite us."

Lady Conyngham looked startled. Andrew stiffened. Exactly what rumor had Lady Conyngham heard? Had she expected Bridget to arrive with straw in her hair? Or wearing her leather breeches? He swallowed a smile. Now *that* would give them something to talk about! Bridget prancing through the drawing room in breeches and boots!

He finished his greeting and led Bridget away through the throng.

"How do they hear each other?" Bridget asked. "I mean there's so terribly much noise. It gives me the headache already."

Andrew sighed heavily. Would the *ton* and its ways never be understandable to her? He was getting quite tired of explaining all the niceties of life. "Remember when I told you about riding in Hyde Park? About how people of the *ton* go there more to be seen than to ride?"

She nodded, her forehead furrowing in a little frown that said clearly that she was trying hard to understand this bewildering new world.

"Well, a soiree's rather like that," he explained. "You really don't come to one to talk or even to eat the food. You come to be seen."

Bridget shook her head, setting her bright curls bouncing. "Andrew, I don't understand *why*. What is so terribly important about being *seen?*"

Andrew sighed again. When she put it that way—as though they were all just being childish—he didn't know how to answer her. He was aware that in a way what he told her didn't make much sense. Being married to her, answering her continual questions, had already made him see things in a new and sometimes startling way. The truth was until now he had done what he was supposed to do—and never bothered to question why. They all did.

He led Bridget through the crowd toward the laden table of food. He would get her a glass of punch and something to eat. Bridget had a healthy appetite—she could always appreciate food, even these delicacies that were unfamiliar to her palate.

Then, as soon as he judged they'd stayed long enough to serve politeness, he could suggest they go home. He didn't think she'd mind that. She was not a person who enjoyed having a great many people around her. Horses now, that would be different. The more horses the better pleased Bridget would be.

As they got closer, he saw that the crowd around the refreshment table was dense. Rather than take her into that crush, he found her a place against the wall, out of the way. "Here," he said, smiling down at her. "You'd best wait here while I get you something to eat and drink."

She shrugged her pale shoulders. "Certainly, Andrew. Whatever you say."

From the look of near exasperation on her face, she was determined to make the best of a bad thing. He supposed they must seem strange, the ways of people who didn't have to work, people that Bridget no doubt felt were useless. But he couldn't help that. Even if she were right in her disdain for the rich who lived on the labor of the poor, he was not the one responsible for the situation. He hadn't chosen to be wealthy; he'd been born into it. And he certainly hadn't chosen to become a marquess.

In fact, he'd fought against it, causing his poor

mother unnecessary pain. Thinking of that, he frowned. The tragedy of Tom's death had been so hard on her— and then to have a son who refused to take up the mantle of authority, who didn't want to assume his rightful place. . . . Thank goodness he'd finally been convinced to do what she wanted, to accept the title. So at least her last days had been peaceful ones—or as peaceful as they could be since her favorite's death had broken her tender heart.

He filled a plate with delicacies for Bridget. Strange, that in a few short days the girl had become so important to him. He'd liked her before, of course, when she'd been just a girl in a stable who liked to talk horses. Then she'd been amusing, easy to talk to. And not at all like a woman.

No, that wasn't entirely the truth. He'd always been aware of Bridget as a woman; he'd just tried to ignore it. To treat her like a man. To talk to her like a man. He talked to her now the same way he had then, but it was different, *he* was different. Because now she was his wife. Already he could hardly remember what his life had been like without her.

Holding the plate high, he started back toward her, wending his way through the multitude. Sidestepping a bull-necked colonel in a too-tight uniform, he almost tipped the glass of punch he was carrying down the décolletage of an elderly lady in bright blue satin with a bejeweled, ostrich-plumed turban perched atop her purple-tinted hair.

"Excuse me." He offered the dowager his best smile and received a half grimace and cold stare in return. So much for the dashing smile for which he'd once been known throughout the city of London. The unfamiliar duties of the title had kept him away from the ladies too long. He must be losing his touch.

He resumed his progress toward his wife. Bridget had remained where he left her, but she was no longer alone. Lady Linden, in a gown of flaming red silk, pressed close to her. From the look of revulsion on Bridget's face—too close.

He glanced around but he didn't see the stickish Linden daughter. She was probably off inventorying the contents of the Conynghams' mansion. But several other ladies were also clustered around Bridget, listening, he supposed, to Lady Linden's latest tattle.

Evading several people and threading his way around some more, he lost sight of Bridget for a moment. He emerged some five feet from the group to see her waving an enthusiastic hand in time to her words.

"Horses are wonderful creatures," she was saying, her tone defensive. "Actually, they make much better friends than people."

"My dear girl." He recognized Lady Linden's falsely sweet tones. "Don't be ridiculous. Horses can't talk. They are dumb beasts."

"Exactly," Bridget said, with fine irony. "Perhaps that is why I prefer them."

A snort from Lady Linden presaged a spate of indignant words ready to pour from her pursed red mouth. But Andrew inserted his body between her bulk and that of another lady and said, "Bridget, my dear, I've brought you those refreshments."

Bridget sent him a look of gratitude which he felt was for much more than food. "Thank you, Andrew. This looks delicious."

He took her elbow. "If you'll excuse us, Lady Linden. There's someone I want Bridget to meet."

Lady Linden faltered, her fat face screwing up in consternation at the thought of her prey being taken away. "But I—"

He didn't wait to hear any more, but expertly maneuvered Bridget out through the crowd, as far from the old gossipmonger as he could get.

"Thank you again," Bridget said around a mouthful of ham. "That woman drives me mad. Why, I almost feel sorry for that horrible daughter of hers. Can you imagine that!"

He smiled. "I don't blame you. I don't quite know how she got so much power. But the elite seem to thrive on her gossip. She has entrée to every drawing room in London, even the finest."

"They don't have enough to do," Bridget said firmly, her even white teeth crunching down on a crispy cracker. "If they had something to *do,* if they had to work for their food, they'd be too busy to lounge about tearing people's lives and reputations to shreds." She nodded, choosing another delicacy from the plate. "That's it, Andrew," she went on with conviction, "people like Lady Linden must be made to work."

That idea—about as feasible as her earlier suggestion that the lady in question be shrunk and put on display—almost sent him off into whoops of laughter. Bridget saw things in such simple terms—the practical approach of a woman used to the rough, straightforward life of the stables.

Bridget was a *doer.* She always would be. And she had short shrift for the lazy dilettantish life of society.

But it wasn't that simple. The verbal muck that Lady Linden threw couldn't be cleaned away, shoveled into a dung pile like the horse manure that Bridget was used to dealing with. Lady Linden's filth stuck in the mind, tainting every thought.

"Who did you want me to meet?" Bridget asked, wiping her mouth daintily with a napkin and then sipping at the punch.

"Ah—" Actually, he hadn't had anyone in mind. He'd only wanted to get his wife away from the huge gossipmonger and her slimy tales. He looked quickly around. Over there. "I want you to meet Wellington."

Bridget's face registered shock. "You mean you want me to meet the *Duke* of Wellington?"

"Yes. The Duke of Wellington."

"But—But," she protested, "I don't know anything about talking to a duke. What should I say?"

Andrew chuckled. "Bridget, my dear. You just read me a panegyric on the lazy ways of the rich and now you're nervous about talking to a mere duke?"

She flashed him a look of disdain. "Don't rag on me, Andrew. Whatever her title, Lady Linden is just an old gossip. She's no better than any village fishwife. But Wellington—" Her eyes shone. "He's a great man. He beat Napoleon at Waterloo."

Andrew smiled. He would never understand his wife. "Come then, and meet the great man."

When she made no more protests, he set her empty plate aside and led her through the assembly.

Wellington saw them coming. "Andrew! Good to see you!" He smiled at them. "And this is your new wife. I heard you'd married."

"Yes, Your Grace. My wife, Bridget."

Wellington reached for Bridget's gloved hand and raised it gallantly to his lips. She stared at it for a moment, as though doubting that he had actually touched her. Then she murmured, "Your Grace."

"I'm pleased to meet such a lovely lady," Wellington said graciously. "Andrew, you've chosen well."

"I think so," Andrew replied, amused. This shy Bridget was one he'd seldom encountered.

Wellington turned back to her. "I hear that you have a marvelous stallion. Named for our victory at Waterloo, isn't he?"

"Yes, your Grace. My father and I raised him. My father's Victor Durabian. He has a stable outside London. Waterloo's a chestnut. By King Midnight, out of Queen Sheba. Excellent pedigree. And he's the fastest horse I've ever seen. He's got the most beautiful—"

Andrew turned to stare at her. The shy anxious Bridget of a moment ago had been transformed. Of course, he thought, Wellington had sensed her edginess and moved to dispel it. He *was* a great man.

"Perhaps I could see him," Wellington interjected when Bridget stopped for breath. "Also I'd like to know your theory about training horses."

"It's easy," Bridget said, stepping closer and laying an urgent hand on the great man's arm. "You just become friends with them. That's all it takes. Even the highest-mettled bloods." She leaned closer still. "Horses are incredibly loyal animals, you know. They'll do anything for you."

He laughed. "But how do you make them your friend?"

"You get acquainted—by blowing your breath into their nostrils. That's the way horses do it. And it works for people, too."

She glanced down, saw where her hand lay on his sleeve, and pulled it back like she'd been burned.

Wellington chuckled. "It's all right, my dear. You've made an old man feel young again. Thank you."

Bridget blushed, the pink traveling from her throat up to her cheeks. "Your Grace, I—"

"There's no need to apologize," Wellington said with a smile. "I love horses, too. Perhaps I'll come round this week to see this wonder." He turned to Andrew again. "If that's agreeable with you."

"Of course." Bridget's advent into society couldn't have a better champion than the national hero of the struggle against Napoleon. "We'd be honored to have you."

Taking Bridget's arm again, Andrew turned away— and came face to face with Wichersham. The man was dressed like a tulip of the turf, but he looked almost ridiculous.

Andrew sensed rather than felt Bridget's sudden tension. Apparently she didn't like Wichersham any more than he did.

"Haverly!" the man said, his tone brisk. "I've been wanting to talk to you."

"Indeed," Andrew replied dryly. "I can't imagine that we have anything to talk about."

He started to move away, Bridget clinging to his arm, but Wichersham moved, too, purposely putting himself in their way. Andrew felt his anger rising. He looked the man over. Wichersham was short with a big gut. His protruding eyes and raspy voice made many people uncomfortable in his presence. But it was not the man's looks, ugly as they might be, that made Andrew wish to get away from him. It was the knowledge that Wichersham had deliberately bought up Durabian's IOUs with the intent of ruining the man. *That* made being civil quite difficult. But he must do it. He gritted his teeth and kept silent; Wichersham was a worm, the lowest of the low. But he couldn't do anything about it—at least not right then.

Andrew pulled in a deep breath. Better steady himself, better be careful. He didn't want Bridget to suspect that Wichersham was the one who'd meant to send her father to debtor's prison. It wouldn't serve any good purpose to give her that information—and knowing her temper, it might do quite a lot of harm.

He straightened and gave Wichersham a quelling look. "Stand aside. We wish to get through."

But Wichersham ignored his request, smiling, a slight curving of thin-pressed lips that imparted a sinister look to his blotchy face. Then he turned his bulging eyes on Bridget. Andrew felt her stiffen, but she didn't let the scoundrel intimidate her. She met his gaze squarely.

"You're looking well, Bridget," Wichersham said unctuously. When he reached out for her free hand, Andrew quickly drew it back, covering it with his own. This slime wasn't going to touch her, not even her glove. Not while her husband was anywhere near.

Wichersham looked from Bridget's face to Andrew's, his expression disparaging. Then he shook his head. "Very well, Haverly. But you'd better tell your—wife—to be kind to me."

"Kind?" Andrew repeated, letting his voice reflect his

incredulity if not his anger. "Why should *Lady Haverly* pay any attention to you at all?"

Wichersham's snide smile made Andrew's hackles rise. The fellow was presuming too far.

"Bridget and I are friends of longstanding," Wichersham purred. "It's—"

"That's a lie!" The words burst from Bridget, making heads near them turn. "A damnable lie!"

Wichersham snickered. "Now, my dear. Don't worry. Surely your new husband will forgive you your past sins. And we can go on being *friends.*"

The emphasis on the last word carried intentional insult, so that Andrew had to swallow hard to contain the curses that rose to his lips. He turned to Bridget; her face was turning crimson. "Andrew, I didn't! You can't—"

He increased the pressure of his fingers over hers. "It's all right, Bridget. No one would believe such a thing." What he'd like to do was give the man a good facer. Stretch him right out on the floor where he belonged. Maybe draw a little blood in the process. For a moment he let himself contemplate the satisfying picture of Wichersham flat on his back, bleeding profusely. He swallowed again. He really shouldn't make a scene, not here where everyone could see. But still, he was sorely tempted.

"Wichersham," Wellington said, stepping out from behind Bridget. "May I speak to you a moment?"

Wichersham was plainly torn—uncertainty written large across his face. Then he evidently decided it wasn't wise to ignore the great man, who could, after all, do a great deal for him if he chose. "I'll speak to you later," Wichersham said, leaning toward Bridget. He moved off, following Wellington into a nearby corner.

Bridget remained silent. Andrew could feel her body trembling against his arm, but her face was expressionless. When they were out of hearing, she said, "Andrew, when can we go home?"

He debated for a moment. Her tone was firm, but he felt her tension. Would their early departure cause more talk, talk they could ill afford? "Bridget, I don't know—"

Why did she respond to Wichersham's fabrications with such vehemence? Surely she didn't think anyone would believe his lies. He knew Bridget would never give herself to the likes of Wichersham.

He patted her hand again. "It's all right, Bridget. He's just trying to worry you." He gazed down into her harried eyes. "But tell me, why are you so upset?"

Her eyes clouded over. "Oh Andrew, I hate that man. He—He tried to—" Her cheeks reddened even more. "Before—at the stables—he cornered me, he wanted me to—"

"I'll kill him!" If the words bursting from his mouth startled him, they turned Bridget pale.

"Andrew, please, don't say such things."

"I mean it," he said fiercely. "If he comes near you, if he offers you any insult, any insult at all, I'll call him out. I'll kill him—I swear it."

"But dueling! Andrew, you can't! They'll arrest you."

"Nonsense," he said, injecting confidence into his tone. "The King doesn't know *what's* going on. And Prinny doesn't care."

Bridget clung to his arm. "But I care. I don't want you to be in danger."

"Come," he said, hugging her words to him. "I am in no danger now. Let us go home."

Chapter Thirteen

The next morning, Bridget woke early. Andrew had been kind after the soiree, assuring her that he didn't believe Wichersham's base innuendoes. As though she would ever let a man like that near her! No man but Andrew had ever touched her—not like that anyway. Still, she'd been very upset, very angry, to think that Wichersham even dared to say such a thing.

She glanced at the clock and threw back the covers. Time for her morning ride. Elsie would be waiting on her corner, two of her prettiest nosegays kept back for her lady.

Bridget hurried into her breeches and boots, tucking in her shirt on the way to the door. First a short trip through the kitchen to pick up Elsie's bread and meat, which Cook now wrapped routinely every morning. And then they would be on their way.

Andrew had gone into his room about an hour earlier, as he usually did at sunup every morning. She hadn't yet told him about her early morning rides. She'd thought about telling him—oh, several times—but somehow she'd just never gotten round to it. Anyway, he wouldn't mind.

She hurried down the stairs, nodded pleasantly to Cook, and hurried out to the stable, Elsie's bread and meat tied in a clean linen cloth that she could slip over her wrist.

Ned would be waiting, his mount and Waterloo saddled and ready.

Sometime later Andrew met Peter at White's. His friend was looking rather down at the mouth. Andrew frowned. Surely Peter hadn't been betting on races—or mills—again. He'd sworn he'd learned his lesson last time.

Andrew slid into his chair. "You look in the dismals. Something wrong?"

Peter shoved aside the remains of his breakfast. "Rather."

Andrew sighed. "Tell me what it is. I'll do what I can to help."

Peter raised an eyebrow. "I'm afraid it's yourself who needs the help."

Andrew put a hand to his head. "It's Bridget, isn't it? Something more about Bridget."

Peter nodded. "Yes, my friend." He smiled slightly. "If you'll recall, I did warn you she'd likely mean trouble."

Andrew groaned. "I know. Well, tell me. What's the story now? What are they prattling about?"

Peter finished off his muffin. "It's all over town. Spread by the Lindens, no doubt. Everyone's talking about your *filly*."

Andrew sighed even louder. "That's no news. What are they *saying?*"

"Well." Peter smiled over the rim of his cup. "They're saying that Bridget isn't fit to be a lady. That all she knows is horses. That she's more fit to be an ostler than a marchioness."

Andrew cursed, long and fluently. "I might have know. Last night she told Lady Linden—and a bunch of other dowagers—that horses make better friends than people. *Because* they can't talk."

Peter grinned. "Actually a very acute observation. But if she said it to Lady Linden, no wonder the tale spread."

Andrew helped himself to a muffin. "Peter, what am I going to do? She continually asks me questions."

"Questions?" Peter looked puzzled. "Questions about what?"

"She wants to know *why* we do things. *Why* we ride in Hyde Park. *Why* we go to soirees. *Why* it's important to be seen. Why, why, why." He groaned again. "I tell you, Peter, she's driving me crazy."

"Hmmm." Peter stared thoughtfully into his cup. "There must be a way out of this bumble broth. Bridget has a fine intellect. There's no reason she can't learn our ways."

"I suppose not." Andrew sipped his tea. "But it's a very time-consuming business. I can't teach her all that she needs to know and still attend to my estate duties. There must be some other way."

"You could hire someone," Peter suggested tentatively.

Andrew snorted. "I don't think Bridget would take kindly to having a governess. You know her, she's the independent sort."

"Very independent," Peter said with another grin. "Let me think." He finished off the last muffin, then snapped his fingers. "I have it! A relative! You must have some female relative, some old dragon who knows it all. Fetch her in for a while and let her teach Bridget the whats and wherefores."

"Hmmm." Andrew thought hard. "You may be right. But who on earth can I get? All my relatives are in the country."

"Who was that aunt you used to tell me about, your mother's sister?"

"Aunt Sophronia!" Andrew sat up straighter, seeing a ray of hope. "That's it! Aunt Sophie is just the one."

"Then I suggest you send for her," Peter said. "The sooner you stop the Lindens' mouths—or at least give them less to say—the better."

Bridget came back from her ride with mixed feelings. She was glad to know that Elsie was getting at least some food in her stomach every day. But every time Bridget looked at the nosegays—one she kept in her bedchamber and one in her sitting room—she thought of the mother-less child out there in London's cruel streets. *She* knew what it meant to be without a mother's love. But at least she'd had Papa. Elsie had no one but a little sister. There must be something more, some better way to help the child.

Bridget washed and changed into a new morning gown of sea foam green, ate her breakfast, and settled down with her needlepoint. More than once as the minutes ticked by she was tempted to curse at pricked fingers or tangled yarn, but she kept her silence, determined to master the knack of this thing. If some *lady* could do it, she could, too.

After all, she told herself, sucking on yet another punctured finger. Andrew had been very good to her. And this at least was a lady's activity she could do alone—without laboring under the blistering stares of those old society matrons. It was hard to understand how anyone so utterly useless, anyone who produced nothing at all in the way of work, could be convinced they knew so much. But they were convinced. And so it seemed, was the rest of the *ton*.

Last night those ladies, who had never been closer to a horse than a seat in a carriage, had declared that horses were "dumb beasts" and marveled at her wanting to associate with them. Dumb indeed! The horses she'd known all had had more intelligence than those ridiculous ladies.

Bridget thought with longing of the stable and its comforting atmosphere, but no, she had promised herself she would give the rest of the morning to this infernal embroidering business—and that was what she meant to do.

She was worrying another length of hopelessly tangled yarn, her tongue caught between her teeth in exasperation, when the door opened. She looked up. "Andrew! I didn't know you were home."

"I just came in," he said, giving her a smile and looking so handsome her heart did a little jump. "So, what are you about there?"

She sighed. "I am trying to learn embroidery, but it's quite fatiguing. The yarn gets all tangled. And I prick my fingers so often."

When she extended a finger to show him, he crossed the room and pulled up a chair beside her. "Let me see," he said, taking her hand gently in his own.

"Dear, dear." He lifted it to his lips and put a gentle kiss on each prick. "You must be quite determined to become an excellent needlewoman." His smile was teasing. "Else why would you undergo such torture?"

"Mrs. Purvey said all ladies embroider," Bridget explained, letting her hand remain comfortably in his. "So I wanted to learn." She lowered her gaze from his face, looking instead at their entwined hands. She liked the way they looked, joined like that. "I know you want me to be a lady. I want to please you."

His fingers tightened around hers in a satisfying squeeze. "You *do* please me," he said in a tone that made her lift her gaze once more to his face. "You please me very much. But you needn't do needlework to achieve that. Only embroider if you feel so inclined."

"Thank you, Andrew." He was looking at her so warmly. Perhaps this was the time to tell him. "You know—"

"There are other things you can learn to do," he went on. "Watercolors. Playing the harpsichord. Things like that. In fact, I've sent for someone to help you do just that."

"Sent?" she mumbled, her heart falling to her toes. Now what was going on?

"Yes. I've sent someone to fetch my Aunt Sophronia. She knows her way about the *ton* and she can answer all your questions."

Bridget withdrew her hand. Oh no! He was going to bring in some withered old harridan to order her about. Or another Lady Linden. "Andrew, I really don't need—"

His handsome face took on the stubborn look she'd come to recognize—and dread, because it meant she had no recourse but to do as he wanted. "I think you'll like Aunt Sophronia."

Sophronia! Bridget suppressed a shudder. She'd been right. Some fat old dragon as bad as that horrible Lady Linden. This was *not* the time to talk about her morning rides or to ask Andrew to do something to help Elsie. That would have to wait for later.

She swallowed hard. "When—When will she get here?"

"Soon," Andrew said. "In a day or two, I hope. Don't worry, my dear, you'll soon know all the ins and outs of life in the *ton*." He smiled. "You'll be able to give the cut direct as well as the next lady."

Bridget swallowed another sigh. She really didn't know why she should *want* to be rude to anyone, except possibly the Lindens. And what was the point of *that*? It wasn't very likely that any amount of rudeness would prevent Lady Linden from inserting her presence wherever she pleased, whether it was wanted or not. But it was apparent that Andrew had made up his mind. She would have to abide by his decision.

After all, she still had her horses—and her early morning ride. She wouldn't—she couldn't—give that up.

The butler appeared in the doorway, clearing his throat.

Andrew looked up. "Yes, Purvey."

"The Duke of Wellington, milord."

"Show him in."

Bridget turned eagerly. She hadn't dared think about what he'd said for fear it wouldn't happen, but the great man had really come. She shoved her needlework down in its basket, smoothed anxiously at her skirt, and raised a nervous hand to her hair.

Andrew laughed. "No need to primp, my dear. You look fine. Delectable as ever."

He turned toward the door where the duke was just coming in. "Wellington, welcome. We're glad to see you."

"I'm glad to be here," Wellington said, smiling at her. She hadn't imagined it. The great man really did like her.

"I'm eager to get a look at the superb creature you call Waterloo," he said. "By King Midnight, out of Queen Sheba, I believe you said."

Bridget got to her feet. "Yes, Your Grace. I'm sure you'll like him."

It was at least an hour later when the duke made his goodbyes. He had exclaimed over Waterloo's wonderful lines and superb confirmation so much that for a time Bridget had forgotten Andrew's discouraging news. But when the duke left, all her doubts came back to trouble her.

As the door closed behind the duke, she turned to her husband. "Andrew, about that aunt of yours—"

"Her name is Sophronia," Andrew said, the stubborn look sliding back over his face. "She was my mother's favorite sister. I'm sure she can teach you the ways of the *ton*. Everything you need to know."

She knew she was fighting a losing battle, but still she had to say it. "I don't see why I must learn anything. I'm not rude. I don't hurt anyone. Why can't people accept me the way I am?"

Andrew sighed heavily. "Some people will, Bridget.

People like Wellington. But others won't. There are conventions to adhere to. And if you don't conform to them, you'll be the talk of the town."

She shrugged. "I'm the talk of the town anyway." She was sorry about that, but it wasn't her fault. It was Lady Linden's. "Why, Andrew? Do you know why Lady Linden should want to hurt me? I've never done a thing to her."

But Andrew couldn't tell her. He could only make empty excuses, excuses that even a child wouldn't believe. And so she resigned herself to the dragon's arrival. At least she still had her horses.

Chapter Fourteen

Bridget spent an anxious few days waiting for the old dragon to arrive. Every morning, of course, she went for her ride, taking food to Elsie and buying the two nosegays the child kept back for her. But every day Bridget's worry grew. The child looked so peaked. There must be some way to get her off the streets, out of that horrible life.

On the afternoon of the third day, Bridget sat restlessly in her sitting room. In spite of Andrew's words, she had not given up her attempt to finish a proper needlepoint design. She'd never been a quitter. And after all, how hard could it be to put a few stitches decently into a piece of material?

So she was sitting there, pulling out still another misshapen stitch, when Purvey appeared in the doorway. "His Lordship's aunt has arrived, milady."

Bridget put down her sewing and got to her feet. "Have you sent to inform him?"

"His Lordship's carriage is right behind hers," Purvey said, his expression bland.

"Very well." Bridget swallowed a sigh. "I'll be right

there." It was really unkind of Andrew to bring someone else into the house. Bad enough that she had to face Lady Linden's badgering. Though now, since Andrew had explained the matter to her, she had no qualms about declaring herself "not at home" when the Lindens came to call.

But she wouldn't be able to evade Andrew's aunt that easily. Sophronia. What kind of name was that for a woman? It sounded like—like some kind of strange disease.

Bridget reached the front hall just as the door opened. She braced herself, ready to face the dragon. Andrew came in, on his arm a beautiful lady dressed in the height of fashion. Bridget stared. Purvey had obviously made a mistake. Where was the old harridan? Why had Andrew brought this woman here?

"Bridget," Andrew called gaily. "Come and meet Aunt Sophronia.

Bridget stared. It was hard to think of this exquisite woman as anyone's aunt. On her small delicate fingers she wore several rings: a wedding ring, a ruby, and an enormous emerald. With her dark dark hair and pansy eyes, she looked like an actress. Or one of those *other* women, the ones men spent so much time with but never talked about—except to each other. Still, Andrew ought to know his own aunt. She moved toward them. "Aunt— Aunt Sophronia?"

"Please call me Aunt Sophie." Her voice was sweet and mellow. "I understand the *ton* has been a little difficult for you." She smiled. "But don't worry. I have been through the whole thing. It's not as difficult as it looks."

"It's not that it's so difficult," Bridget found herself saying. "It's that it doesn't make any sense."

Oh dear, now she'd insulted Andrew's aunt. But to her surprise the stranger laughed, a delightful sound, like the tinkling of many little bells.

"My dear Bridget," she said cheerfully. "That is precisely your problem. You mustn't expect *sense*. Not at all. You learn the whole thing, all by rote. And then you do it, *without* thinking."

Bridget shook her head. "That doesn't make sense either."

Aunt Sophie laughed merrily and Andrew laughed with her. For a moment Bridget felt a surge of irritation at both of them. These *tonnish* people had some peculiar ways of looking at life.

She moved closer. She could at least be polite to Andrew's relative. "I'm glad to meet you, Aunt Sophie. And I appreciate your coming to help me. I'll try to be a good learner."

Andrew smiled at her, giving her that warm feeling inside, the feeling that made her glad he was her husband. "I know you'll do your best, my dear," he said. And she wanted to—she wanted to please him.

Aunt Sophie looked at Andrew. "And now if I may—"

"Aunt Sophie?" Bridget asked. She knew Andrew's aunt was probably tired from her trip, but she really needed to know.

"Yes, Bridget?"

"Do you know how to embroider?"

"Of course," she said, sending Andrew a look of amazement. "Do you want me to help you with yours?"

"Yes," Bridget replied with relief. "And—And do you like horses?"

"I love them," Aunt Sophie said brightly, waving a beringed hand, "especially when they're racing! It's so terribly exciting."

"Oh, how marvelous," Bridget cried. "I think we shall deal well together."

"I think so, too," Aunt Sophie said with a smile. "Yes, I think so, too."

By the next afternoon when the two sat together over Bridget's stitching, they had already become great friends. They had spent an enjoyable morning discussing gowns and bonnets, dinner parties and dances. With much laughter and fun, Aunt Sophie had instructed Bridget in the intricacies of the waltz. But when, after some hilarious attempts, she declared her pupil competent to accept any partner, Bridget had frowned and said, "I don't know that I want just *any* partner. It seems an improper sort of dance."

Aunt Sophie grinned. "No more improper than riding through London's streets in leather breeches."

Bridget felt the color rising in her cheeks. "How—How did you know?"

"Mrs. Purvey," Aunt Sophie said. "She has glimpsed you on the stairs more than once. But she didn't feel it her place to tell Andrew about it." Aunt Sophie frowned a little, pulling at a stitch. "She's worried about you, Bridget. It seems that your morning rides are becoming common knowledge. Servants talk, too, you know."

Bridget sighed. "I don't believe I'll ever get the knack of this *tonnish* business. There's so much to learn." She pushed at a straggling wisp of hair. "Tell me, Aunt Sophie, what harm does it do for me to ride? No one is about at that hour. The park is quite empty."

Aunt Sophie put down her stitching. "You're right, my dear, your riding harms no one. But the *ton* feels it has the right to control its members." She sighed even louder and began twisting her wedding ring. "And if you go against its wishes, you will be sorry. I know."

The last words were spoken with such sadness that Bridget leaned forward impulsively. "Aunt Sophie, what happened to you?"

Aunt Sophie laughed, a sound of great melancholy. "What always happens, I suppose. I loved a man, a man of the wrong class." She sighed. "And my family would not hear of my marrying him. So I ran away to Gretna Green and married him anyway. There was a tremendous scandal. I was cut by everyone—for a long time." She straightened. "He has been dead some years now."

"Oh Aunt Sophie, I'm so sorry. It was kind of you to come back to the city to help me."

"It was all long ago," Aunt Sophie said, stitching industriously and not looking up. "The *ton* has long since had other tattle to whisper about."

"Still—"

Purvey appeared in the doorway. "Lady Linden, milady, and her daughter."

Bridget smiled. "Tell them I'm not—"

"And the Duke of Wellington."

"Oh no! She turned to Aunt Sophie. "Now what shall I do?"

"I'm afraid we'll have to receive all our callers or none," Aunt Sophie said with a wicked smile.

Bridget sighed. "Show our guests in." She couldn't turn the duke away. That would be too rude.

"Imagine." Lady Linden began speaking even before she was entirely through the door. "Imagine who we met just outside!"

She came sweeping in wearing a gown of carnelian satin adorned with row upon row of stiff ruching. After her came the daughter, in her usual drab grayish green, her person and her gown entirely devoid of ornamentation. And immediately behind the two of them strode the duke, his military bearing in great contrast to their feminine persons.

"Good day," the duke said. "I hope I won't interfere with your other guests." The twinkle in his eye told Bridget that he was aware of the predicament his arrival had caused her.

"Indeed not," she said. "Do sit down."

The duke nodded, but before he seated himself, he bowed before Aunt Sophie, raising her hand to his lips. "Sophronia. I heard you were in town. You're looking lovely as ever."

A slight flush rose to Aunt Sophie's cheeks. Evidently these two had known each other before. For a moment Bridget wondered how well.

Then the duke turned to her. "You're looking lovely, too, Lady Haverly. Your usual delightful self."

He nodded briefly to the other two and settled into a chair.

It was a most instructive afternoon. As the time passed, Bridget watched the duke skillfully sidestep every effort of the Lindens to spread gossip or blacken anyone's good name. Before she had thought him a great man, now she also thought him a good one.

In his presence Aunt Sophie seemed to sparkle. Lady Linden, however, looked almost deflated—like one of those French air balloons that had crashed and was losing all its gas. Without the gossip that was her stock in trade, she could scarcely function.

"So," the duke asked finally. "How is that wonderful stallion of yours? You still think he's the fastest thing on four legs?"

Bridget grinned. "Of course I do. He won against Sable, didn't he? He can beat any horse living."

The duke smiled, a demon of mischief lurking in his eyes. "Are you sure?"

"Quite sure," Bridget replied, sitting up straighter. "Why do you ask?"

The duke settled back expansively. "Oh, I've acquired a new stallion—better tempered than Copenhagen. A rousing boy he is. I'd like to see him run against a *real* horse. See what he can do."

Bridget leaned forward. "His name, Your Grace. What's his name?"

"Blackberry," the duke said. "Inelegant name for an animal, but at least original."

"Blackberry," Bridget repeated. "By Cobblestone, out of Lady May."

The duke nodded, his eyes bright. "You've seen him run?"

"Yes." Bridget was aware of the disdainful looks the Lindens were exchanging, but she didn't care. Here at last was something *she* enjoyed talking about. "He's a little short in the withers, but a good horse."

"But he can't beat Waterloo?" the duke persisted.

"Of course not. I told you, no horse—"

"Then you wouldn't mind a race?"

Bridget's heart jumped up in her throat. Mind! She'd love it. Racing was the most exciting thing. "Any day in the week," she said. But common sense raised its head, if only for a moment. How would Andrew feel about this? Proper, proper Andrew. A glance at Aunt Sophie showed that her eyes were sparkling like the duke's. Bridget swallowed. "But are you sure Andrew won't mind?"

"Of course," the duke said. "What harm can there be in a little friendly competition?" He smiled. "Which of Andrew's men will ride for you?"

"None," Bridget said. "I shall ride him myself."

The gasp that issued from Lady Linden's red mouth turned all their heads. "Yourself?" she squeaked. "Oh dear. Oh dear!"

Bridget flushed. Was she always to be getting herself into the suds? Well, it was too late to back out of this now.

"Do you care to make a small wager on the side?" the duke asked, his smile devilish.

Bridget shook her head. "No, Your Grace. I don't wager. It's a dangerous habit."

For a moment, looking deep into his eyes, she thought that he *knew*, that somehow he had discovered the wager that had made her Andrew's wife. But that couldn't be. No one but the four of them—Papa, Andrew, Peter, and herself—knew. And none of them would tell.

"Well then," the duke said. "It only remains to set the time and place."

"The time and place for what?" Andrew inquired from the doorway. It appeared he'd returned home just in time.

Something was going on, something he didn't like the feel of. The Lindens looked about to explode with a surfeit of information. And Aunt Sophie, Bridget, and Wellington were all bright-eyed and eager.

"Your wife has agreed to race Waterloo against my Blackberry," Wellington said.

Andrew frowned. "I see." Some help Aunt Sophie was. Why hadn't she stopped this thing?

"It was entirely my idea," Wellington went on. "I wish to see how well he can do against the best. And Waterloo *is* the best."

That was true enough. But a race . . .

"Do you prefer Tattersall's or your father's track?" Wellington asked Bridget.

"It doesn't matter," she said. "I'll leave that up to you."

"Let's make it Tattersall's then. Neutral ground, so to speak."

Bridget nodded. "Fine."

"And how about Tuesday week? One in the afternoon?"

"Fine again," Bridget said, her face all aglow. Horses! Horses always made her light up like that.

"You won't back out?" Wellington said. "You'll be there as promised?"

"Of course!" Bridget looked almost insulted.

"Of course," Andrew repeated. "Bridget always keeps her word."

Wellington got to his feet. "See?" he told Bridget. "As I said, it was perfectly proper. I'll see you then. I'm looking forward to watching you ride."

And while Andrew stood there in shock, Wellington nodded to the ladies and left.

Lady Linden pulled her bulk erect, though with some little effort. "We must go, too," she chirped, her chins quivering. "Other calls to make, you know. So many calls." And she rolled out, the stickish daughter right behind her.

He managed to contain himself until he heard the front door close behind their guests, then he rounded on the women. "What is the meaning of this?" he yelled, conscious that he was behaving in an unseemly fashion, but unable to stop himself. "He wants to watch Bridget race?"

Aunt Sophie had the grace to look a little sorry, but Bridget stared right back at him. "He told you. The duke wanted a race."

"A race, yes," Andrew blustered. "But that doesn't mean you must—"

"Of course it does," Bridget said, her color high. "I told you, Waterloo's woman's horse. He's come to be friends with Ned, of course. But Ned's not good at racing."

He wanted to give them both a good thrashing, though of course he'd never really strike a woman. "Aunt Sophie, how could you? How could you let such a thing happen?"

She had stopped looking embarrassed and met his gaze squarely. "Be reasonable, Andrew. Would you have Bridget refuse the Duke of Wellington?"

"Of course not." Even in his anger he could see that that couldn't be done. "But she doesn't—"

"Yes, she does," Aunt Sophie said, with that false patience that women use when they think a man unreasonable. "She wants the horse to win. As you should. And so *she* must ride it."

"Women!" Andrew exploded. "You just wait. The Lindens will have this all about town in no time." He glanced at the clock. "I dare say that by now they've already told at least a dozen people."

"Now you are being quite unreasonable," Aunt Sophie said in the tone she used to take when he was a small misbehaving boy. "Neither Bridget nor I is responsible for the Lindens' capacity for gossipmongering. And," she went on before he could open his mouth again, "the duke arrived at the same time they did, so if we were 'at home' to him we had also to be 'at home' to them."

What she said made a certain sense, but she had missed the main point. With the Lindens gabbling about the race, all of fashionable London was apt to show up to see *his* wife in leather *breeches,* riding *astride!*

Chapter Fifteen

The day of the race dawned bright and clear—a blue sky and a warm breeze. Looking at the sun streaming in through the window, Bridget sighed. The day might be sunny, but her heart wasn't.

Andrew had been so different lately. Since the day the duke had set up the race, Andrew seemed always at outs with her, always picking at her. Do this. Don't do that. For several nights he hadn't come to her bed at all.

She'd missed him dreadfully, tossing and turning, unable to sleep. And then, when he had come to her, he'd left in the middle of the night, as though he'd only been there for one thing and once he had it, he couldn't bear to stay with her.

She sighed again. His not being there this morning meant she could get out for her ride in the park, but even that had lost its glow. If it hadn't been for Elsie waiting on her corner, she wouldn't even have gone riding. But Elsie must have her bread and meat, and Bridget must buy her nosegays. Otherwise the child might starve—or just as bad—be beaten by the man who drank up all the money.

She turned on her side. This whole business of the *ton* was quite difficult for her to understand. Whatever was wrong with Andrew? He'd certainly known when he married her what sort of person she was—that horses were her whole life. If he hadn't wanted a wife like that, why had he stuck to the wager? He could have given all kinds of excuses to get out of the marriage, but he hadn't. And there was still something very odd about that race. If only she knew what had made Waterloo lose. He'd never lost a race before then.

She threw back the covers. Well, there was no time to puzzle about races now. Elsie was waiting. And she was hungry.

Later that day, when it was time to leave for the race, Bridget met Aunt Sophie in the front hall. She felt strange to be there in her breeches but she held herself straight. She had nothing to be ashamed of.

Aunt Sophie looked marvelous in a gown of soft blush pink. For the first time Bridget thought with longing of the new gowns in her armoire. *Well,* she told herself with disgust, *you wanted to race. You thought it would be marvelous. So now enjoy it.*

"Have you seen Andrew?" she asked. "Is he coming to watch?"

Aunt Sophie shook her head, twisting her wedding ring as she did when she was nervous. "I'm afraid not. I saw him earlier and he said he was off about some business."

She let her gaze travel over Bridget's breeches and boots. "I can see why he might object to your running around town in such an outfit." She pursed her rosy lips into a pout. "Really, my dear, that getup leaves very little to the imagination."

"Well," Bridget replied. "He must know that I can't ride in a gown. Why, at first I could hardly even walk in one." She stuffed her hair up under her cap. "Tell me, Aunt Sophie, if you know, why is the world so unfair to women?"

Aunt Sophie frowned. "I don't know, Bridget. It's just another of the things that are. We should be grateful that we have men who take care of us and—"

"But that's just it," Bridget cried. "I can do anything my father can. I know more about horses than even he does. He'll tell you that himself."

Aunt Sophie nodded soothingly. "I'm sure he will."

"But that's what is so unfair! What I know doesn't matter! What I know doesn't matter because the instant a man sees I'm female, he starts looking for another man to deal with. If something happened to Papa, I could run the stables. But no one would *let* me."

Aunt Sophie patted her hand. "What can I say? Now come, my dear. We don't want to be late."

"But—"

"It's quite true what you say. But neither you—nor I—can fix it in a day. Or a month, or a year. We can only chip away at the edge of injustice by showing people that we *can* do things. Like you are doing today."

"Yes," Bridget said. Perhaps Aunt Sophie *did* understand. "I'm going to show them. They'll see. I'm going to win."

Tattersall's yard was packed with people, happy, boisterous, fashionable people, all talking about the race, and bookies taking bets. Bridget stood with a hand on Waterloo's neck, gazing out over the great crowd. "All these people," she told him, "have come to see you race. To see you win. And that's what you're going to do. You're going to win."

She stroked his great muscled neck. "You're a marvelous horse, Waterloo. The best and most beautiful horse in all of London."

"So," said a harsh voice behind her. "Still talking to horses, I see."

The cold chill that crept up her spine told her as much as the raspy voice. Bridget turned to face Wichersham, keeping a comforting hand on the stallion's neck. Surely Wichersham wouldn't try anything with so many people around. "What do you want?" she asked, her tone sharp.

His smile made her flesh crawl. "Why, just to wish you good luck," he said.

"She don't need luck. Not from the likes of ye." Papa came from round the corner. "She's got the best horse in London. She knows it and *he* knows it. Don't need no more."

Papa came up on Waterloo's other side and put an arm round his neck, his hand close to Bridget's.

A sneer appeared on Wichersham's face. "Perhaps," he said. "Perhaps not." He gave Papa a look full of menace and moved off into the crowd.

"Don't let him worry ye none," Papa said. "He can't do ye no harm."

"He's a terrible man." Bridget leaned closer to the stallion, taking comfort in his scent, his feel, his very nearness. "I wonder someone hasn't killed him before now."

Papa laughed, a little strained perhaps, but still a laugh. "Now, now, me girl. No doubt there's been men aplenty thinking of it. And him even deserving of it—mayhap. But killing's a mortal sin. And not for the likes of us. Ye know that, now don't ye?"

Bridget turned, looking at him from beneath the stallion's head. "Yes, Papa, I know. But he's such an evil man."

For a minute Papa looked surprised, and anxious. Then when she didn't say any more, he nodded. "That he is, me dear, that he is."

At the back of the crowd, Andrew was berating himself. He had meant to go about his business like this was any ordinary day. He had certainly *not* meant to make an appearance at this ridiculous race. But he'd found himself thinking about the race—indeed, he could think of nothing else—and so finally he had surrendered to the inevitable. Now here he was, trying to hide in the back of this dense mass of people and still see what was going on.

He saw Bridget's father lead her and Waterloo toward the starting line. At the same time Wellington was approaching with his jockey, already up on Blackberry. The horse was a fine-looking beast, about Waterloo's size. He carried himself proudly, too.

For a moment Andrew felt a twinge of anxiety. This might turn out to be a *real* race. He knew Bridget. Winning meant a lot to her. If she lost this race, how would she feel?

Of course, if she lost the race, it might calm her down a bit, might prevent her from accepting any further challenges—and maybe give *him* some peace of mind. But was that what he wanted? Really wanted?

The riders were up; the starter gave the signal. The horses were off.

Andrew craned forward, trying to see over those in front of him. Blackberry pulled ahead by about a nose. And there he stayed, unable to gain any more ground. As the horses pounded round the track, Andrew tried to think as Bridget would think. What was going on inside her head? Was she holding the stallion back till she was ready to make her move? Would she let him go at the last moment and win the race in a great burst of glory? Or was she thinking of Wellington's pride?

The crowd was going crazy, yelling and screaming for their favorites. Some distance away he could see Wellington, laughing with a companion, entirely at ease. Evidently the duke saw nothing wrong with Bridget's behavior. But then, she wasn't *his* wife.

The horses came round the turn on the final lap of the race. Over the heads of the crowd, he could see Bridget lean forward, whispering something into the stallion's cocked ear. The great horse shook his mane. And inch by inch, he pulled steadily ahead.

She was doing it! Bridget was winning the race—and without making Wellington's animal look bad. He felt a surge of pride. She was something, his Bridget. A real winner.

But then, across the throng, he saw a huge orange bonnet and the even greater bulk of Lady Linden in a gown that resembled a carnival tent. He swallowed a curse. That busybody would have her mouth going steadily—she'd already set the city on its ear with her talk—

and now they'd all be gabbling about Bridget in her breeches—and who knew what else.

"There she goes!" Peter cried, appearing at his elbow and clutching his arm in excitement. "She's going to win!"

"Of course," Andrew said, pride overcoming his uneasiness. "Bridget always wins."

"And she has!" Peter clapped him heartily on the back. "Come on, let's go. You'll want to congratulate her."

"I—" Andrew thought of refusing, of making excuses, but with Peter pulling at him, he could hardly disappear back into the crowd. Besides, someone had surely seen him there, someone who would spread it about if he didn't show up at Bridget's side after such a victory. "I'm coming," he said.

Bridget was surrounded by clamoring people, all crowding close, all wanting to congratulate her. The stallion stood still, looking every inch the king. But it was easy to see that the crowd meant nothing to him, all his attention was on Bridget—his mistress, the center of his life.

And she, she stood leaning against him, her arm flung familiarly over his sweaty neck. Andrew swallowed a curse. There was that jealousy again.

"Here, here," Peter cried, using his elbows to push ahead. "Let the triumphant husband through. Make way now, I say."

Bridget turned to them, her lovely face flushed with victory, but when she saw him, Andrew thought anxiety crept into her eyes. "Andrew! I didn't know you were here."

He pulled himself together and managed a smile. "Of

course, I'm here. I wouldn't miss seeing you race. You should know that."

He saw her surprise, and for a moment he thought she'd say something—tell him she hadn't known he'd be there at all. But she masked it quickly, tucking an arm through his and drawing him closer to the horse. "Wasn't he marvelous? He's such a great runner."

"Yes," Andrew said, patting the horse's neck. "He's capital."

"The horse is just an animal." Wichersham shoved his way to the front of the spectators, his blotchy face shining with sweat, his raspy voice grating on all ears. "And not such a great one at that."

Bridget stiffened. "What do you mean? Why, he's the fastest—"

"That's enough," Andrew interrupted, looking Wichersham right in the eye, an uncomfortable sensation rather like sinking into a mudhole. "Your opinion of the horse means nothing to us," he said brusquely. "And now if you'll excuse us."

Wichersham didn't move. His shifty eyes slid over Bridget, resting overlong on the swell of her bosom under the white shirt and then on her leather breeches. Andrew sensed her outrage before he heard it in her angry gasp, felt it in the way she pulled her arm loose from his. He saw that arm swing up, her hand forming a fist—a fist aimed at Wichersham's sneering face.

For a second he wanted to let her do it, let her give the scoundrel the facer he deserved. But that would cause no end of scandal, and Bridget didn't need scandal. Andrew grabbed her arm, stopping the blow in mid-swing. "He's

151

not worth it, Bridget," he said softly. "Don't dirty your hands on such filth. Forget him. He has no class."

"You're right," she said firmly, her voice suddenly regal. "He has no class at all."

"Bridget!" Wellington cried, pushing through the front of the crowd. "An excellent race! Did you see how well Blackberry ran?"

"Yes, Your Grace." Bridget turned her back on Wichersham, extending a hand to Wellington. "He's a fine horse. Waterloo really had to stretch to beat him."

Wellington laughed. "You're too kind," he said. "I suspect you could have won by more." He turned to Andrew. "You're a lucky man, Haverly. A really lucky man."

"I know," Andrew said, the enthusiasm in his voice rather surprising even to him.

It must have surprised Bridget, too, for she turned to him, a great smile lighting her face. "Oh Andrew, I'm lucky, too. To be your wife."

"Why don't we see *you* on the stallion, Haverly?" The voice came from the crowd, but it sounded suspiciously like Wichersham's hard rasp. "Can't you manage him?"

Andrew looked out quickly, searching, but Wichersham's ugly face wasn't evident. He decided the best thing to do was to ignore the remark. He would ride Waterloo soon enough.

He turned back to Bridget, who was busily engaged in talking horse breeding with Wellington. When he got a chance, he'd suggest that he have a go at the stallion. What was that Bridget had said? Something about him being a woman's horse? Ridiculous, of course. There wasn't a horse living he couldn't ride.

"Breeding," Bridget was saying to the duke. "Yes, Your Grace, breeding is important, of course. But it's the training that counts." She lowered her voice. "And the love you give a horse. That's what really does it—the love."

Chapter Sixteen

The next morning Andrew woke early. He had returned to his own bed some hours before because sleeping beside Bridget only reminded him of the problems facing him. He hated having her name bruited about the city. And as for them calling her his *filly* and laying bets as to whether he would tame her, that was sheer foolishness. Bridget was far likelier to tame him—or drive him to complete distraction. He wasn't sure which she would do first.

He sighed and turned toward the window where the rising sun was just beginning to streak the morning sky with pink and gold. Bridget. What a difference she'd made in his life.

On impulse he threw back the covers and slipped into his robe. He'd never gone to her room at dawn, but there was always a first time. He opened the door softly, hoping not to startle her, thinking to slip beneath the covers beside her and wake her in other, more pleasurable ways.

And then he drew in a breath. Bridget wasn't asleep, she was already out of bed, her back to him. Standing on one leg, she had the other halfway into her breeches. Breeches! Why was she putting on breeches?

"Bridget!" he called. "What are you doing?"

At the sound of his voice, she whirled, lost her balance, and started to topple. He rushed forward, catching her just in time for the both of them to end up on the floor in a wild tangle of arms and legs.

"Andrew," she said, disengaging herself from him with some difficulty. "What are you doing here?"

"I—I came to you—to be with you."

"Oh." The word was a mere whisper.

"What are you doing? Why are you wearing these?" His hand slid down to the breeches, lingered there overlong.

She turned her face away. "I—I'm going for my morning ride."

She was avoiding his eyes. A dreadful suspicion snuck into his mind. "Do you—Every morning do you ride—like this—in breeches?"

She straightened, meeting his gaze squarely. "Of course. How else? No one can really ride in a skirt. You should know that. Well, you couldn't *know*, but you could guess."

He nodded. What she said made a certain perverted sense. Another suspicion slithered in to join the first. "Please, don't tell me you ride *alone*."

She cast him a quelling look. "Of course I don't. Ned always goes with me."

Relieved, he expelled a long breath. "Thank the good Lord for that!"

She drew herself erect. "I'm not stupid, Andrew," she said testily. "Don't treat me as though I were."

"Of course not." She seemed a little touchy this morning. He hoped nothing was wrong. He turned toward his door. "Just let me get dressed. I've been wanting to try a ride on the stallion. This morning's as good a time as any, I guess."

She looked about to comment at that, then snapped her mouth shut instead and resumed her dressing.

When they reached the stable, Bridget saw Ned start, then quickly recover. "Morning, yer Lordship," he said humbly. "Will ye be wanting Sable this morning?"

Andrew nodded. "Yes, Ned. Saddle her up, please."

"Aye, yer Lordship. Will ye be wanting me to follow along of ye?"

"Yes, Ned. Attend us. Just as you do her Ladyship."

Bridget swallowed a sigh. Too bad they couldn't leave Ned at home. Andrew wanted to ride Waterloo and he wasn't going to listen to her. She knew what would happen, knew it as well as she knew her own name. Andrew would mount, and Waterloo would unseat him. One way or another he would unseat him.

They reached the park with little conversation between them. Then Andrew pulled up the filly and looked around. "I can see why you like coming here early. It's very pleasant."

"Yes." She managed a smile. "It reminds me somehow of Papa's place."

Andrew smiled, too. "I think I'll have that ride on Waterloo now."

Sighing, Bridget swung down. "You know, Andrew, you ought to get acquainted with him first. Remember, Waterloo doesn't like—"

"Nonsense," he interrupted in that brusque overriding tone she loathed. He swung down easily. "There's no need to get acquainted. The horse knows me. I've been in the stable often enough. Besides, horses always take to me."

"But—"

He didn't wait for the rest of her sentence, but turned Sable over to Ned and took Waterloo's reins from her hands.

When Andrew swung up, Waterloo turned his head, cocking an inquiring eye backward at his rider, an eye that showed the warning of white. Trouble was coming, Bridget knew. Andrew was going to get a big surprise. And soon.

"You see—" Andrew began. But he didn't even get to finish his sentence. Waterloo leaped. Straight up into the air the stallion went, coming down on all four feet so hard that the earth seemed to shake. Twice. Three times.

On the fourth, Andrew bounced right out of the saddle, hitting the turf with a thud—and a muttered curse. But since he was cursing, he must be all right. Bridget went to calm the horse, patting him and murmuring soothing words till he settled down, nuzzling her shoulder and crowding close, almost like he wanted comfort.

By the time she left the horse and reached Andrew, he was struggling to his feet, his face reddening in embarrassment. "Damnation! What in blue blazes is going on?"

Bridget swallowed a sudden urge to giggle but she clamped her teeth together—giggling in this situation would never do. It didn't take much intelligence to know that Andrew wouldn't like being laughed at. She struggled to keep her voice calm. "I tried to tell you, Andrew. It's not you. He just doesn't like males."

"That can't be," Andrew said, dusting off his breeches. "It's simple enough. The horse is just a one-man, that is, a one-woman horse. No one else can ride him."

"That's not true," Bridget insisted. "Any female can ride him. Any female at all."

"Nonsense." Andrew turned back to the filly, grabbing her reins from Ned and swinging hastily up.

She was tired of this arrogance, of him thinking that he knew so much more than she did, especially about horse-flesh. "All right, then how about a wager?"

He turned back, his face curious. "A wager? What kind of wager?"

She chose her words carefully. "I'll show you that I'm right about this. On the way home, we'll stop some child on the street. Some *girl* child. You can even choose her. And if she can ride Waterloo, then I win."

"Win what?"

She thought for a minute. "If I win, you'll listen to me. You'll get acquainted with him the way I say. You'll let me show you how to make friends with a horse."

Andrew laughed in disbelief. "If some child can ride that horse, I'll listen to you all right. You can be sure of that." He laughed again. "But if she can't, then you'll give off saying such ridiculous things. Like a horse being able to tell the gender of its riders."

"Agreed," Bridget retorted. Why must he be so prickly? Couldn't he just believe her?

Andrew grinned, his good humor suddenly restored. "In fact, since it's so impossible, I'll give you an extra incentive."

"What kind of incentive?" she asked, curiosity getting the better of her.

"If you win, you can make one request of me. And I'll grant it. One request. No matter what it might be. I promise."

"Agreed." Obviously he didn't think she had any chance of winning or he would never have said such a foolish thing. Imagine! Anything she wanted. She smiled to herself. Andrew should remember he wasn't so good at the betting game. Last time he'd wagered he'd ended up with a wife.

At his signal, they set off, racing across the park, the two horses side by side. She was careful to keep Waterloo from pulling out in front of the filly. They had a good gallop, an invigorating ride. Bridget relaxed, enjoying the wind in her face, the power of the stallion's great body between her legs. Yes, this was living. A great gallop on a great horse, the man she loved beside her.

After a while, Andrew veered, turning Sable back the way they'd come. And Bridget followed him.

When they reached the place where they'd begun the run, Andrew slowed the filly—and Bridget slowed Waterloo, too.

"Now," he said, turning toward the exit. "Now for the wager."

"All right," Bridget replied. "Now for the wager."

They came out of the park, the horses making their way through the now-crowded streets, weaving among the laboring people, the clerks with their bundles, the shop-girls with their brooms, the chimney sweeps and the crossing sweepers. And they came to the corner where Elsie waited, the huge battered basket of flowers at her bare feet, a nosegay extended in her grimy hand.

"Buy me flowers," she sang out, giving Bridget a smile before she glanced up at Andrew. "Flowers fer the pretty lady?" she asked him.

Andrew glanced down, his face gone serious. "This child," he said. "This child will do fine."

Bridget swallowed hastily. She'd never imagined he'd choose Elsie. Should she tell him that she knew the girl, that she stopped and bought flowers from her every day?

And then it struck her—like a kick from an angry horse. *Anything*, Andrew had said. She could have anything she wanted. My God! If she won her bet, she could . . .

"Very well," she said to him. "Will you do it or shall I?"

Andrew laughed, a sound that, full of sarcasm as it was, raised prickles on her skin. "You can do it," he said. "You're the expert on horses."

And that decided her. If he hadn't been so arrogant, so sure that he knew everything there was to know, she might have told him that she knew Elsie. But he had no right to be so puffed up with his own importance. And he certainly had no right to question her competence with horses. Where horses were concerned, she always knew what she was doing.

"Very well," she said, swinging down. She turned to Elsie, whose smudged face was full of curiosity. "Now child," Bridget said, stressing the word only slightly and hoping Elsie wouldn't spoil things by letting on that they were already friends.

"Yes, lady?" Elsie's eyes shone up at her. She *had* caught on.

Bridget continued. "His Lordship here, my husband, he doesn't think that you can ride the horse."

"That 'orse?" Elsie's smile melted, becoming a small frown. "That big 'orse?"

"Yes," Bridget said. "You see, I've told his Lordship that the horse doesn't like boys."

Elsie nodded. "Nasty things sometimes, boys is. Pulling me 'air and knocking with their fists."

"That's it," Bridget agreed. "But his Lordship doesn't believe me about the horse. He couldn't ride him. I want to prove to him that I'm right. So I want you to get on the stallion. And ride him."

"What 'appened to 'is Lordship when 'e got on?" Elsie demanded apprehensively.

Bridget hesitated. Andrew wasn't going to like this. "He—ah—"

"I hit the ground," Andrew said, looking down at the child with a fierce frown. "I hit the ground hard."

The child looked so frightened that for a moment Bridget thought she would refuse altogether. Then Elsie put the nosegay carefully back into her battered basket and extended a dirty hand to Bridget. "I'll do it, lady. I'll ride the 'orse—fer ye."

"Thank you," Bridget said, squeezing the grimy little fingers. "Now, don't be afraid. You just do like I tell you."

Elsie nodded. "I will, lady. I will."

"First," Bridget said, "come here. Come up to Waterloo's nose."

Elsie stepped up, her little face almost even with the stallion's long muzzle as Waterloo had bowed his head down. " 'E's awful big, ain't 'e?"

"Yes," Bridget said. "But he won't hurt you. Now, lean

forward a little. Blow into his nostrils like this." She blew softly.

Elsie looked skeptical, but she leaned forward, pulled in a breath, and blew. Then she wrinkled her little nose and jumped. "Lordy, lady, 'e blew back at me!"

Bridget chuckled. "He's saying that now he knows you. Now he'll let you ride him."

Elsie still didn't look convinced, but she kept her hand in Bridget's. " 'Ow I gonna get on 'im?" she asked, a little quaver in her voice.

"I'll put you up," Bridget said. "Just like this." And she lifted the child to the horse's back and put the reins in her hands. "Hold them this way. And don't be afraid. I promise that he won't hurt you."

Elsie nodded, looking like she was indeed afraid, but too afraid to open her mouth to say so.

"Back off a way," Andrew said to Bridget. "Of course, he won't do anything when you're standing right there."

"Don't be afraid," Bridget repeated to the child. "He won't hurt you."

When Elsie nodded again, Bridget walked away, around Sable, and out of the stallion's sight.

"Now," she called. "Cluck to him and he'll start to walk. Guide him with the reins. Guide him in a circle."

She peered over the filly's back, almost holding her breath. If only this went well, if Elsie could do it, she would win, and she could ask Andrew . . .

Waterloo walked off, his head high, his gaze steady. He behaved as sedately as if she herself were on his back. Round and round he walked, carrying the child in a circle near them.

Bridget turned and looked at Andrew. "Well? Do I win the wager?"

He frowned, his expression incredulous. "I'll be da— That is, how did you manage this?"

She sighed. It was so simple. "I told you. Waterloo doesn't like boys."

"I suppose *he* told you so," Andrew said, his voice heavy with sarcasm.

"No, he didn't. I know because one day I found some boys chasing him round the far paddock. They took turns till he was tired, they said, and then they rode him into the ground."

"So he doesn't like males." His voice was still skeptical, but not nearly as sarcastic as it had been.

Bridget nodded. "But he will learn to like you if you just let him get acquainted."

Andrew finally grinned. "All right, I stand corrected. I should have known that where horses are concerned there's no way to best you. You know too much."

Bridget grinned, too. "Thank you. It's good to be appreciated." She turned to the child, still guiding the horse in circles. "Stop now."

" 'Ow?" Elsie said. " 'Ow do I stop 'im?"

"Waterloo, whoa," Bridget called. The stallion halted, sending an inquiring look her way and pricking his ears.

She came out from behind the mare and lifted Elsie from his back. "You did very well," she said. "Thank you."

Elsie bent quickly to her basket, bringing up two nosegays. "Buy me flowers?" she asked. "Pretty flowers?"

"Yes," Bridget said. "We'll take two."

While Andrew fished in his pocket for some coins,

Bridget leaned closer to whisper. "Ned will come later with your food."

She gave the child the coins Andrew passed her and swung up on the stallion again. "Shall we go home?" she asked her husband.

"Yes," Andrew said. "And you can be contemplating the nature of the wish you want me to fulfill."

"Very well," Bridget said. "I'll think about it." Actually she wouldn't have to think at all. She knew exactly what she wanted. But this wasn't the time to tell him. She had to lay the groundwork, lay it carefully. And then everything would be just as she wanted it.

Chapter Seventeen

That night Bridget went to the dinner table in a new gown of deep green satin. Pulling out her chair for her, Andrew dropped a kiss on her bare shoulder. "You're looking especially lovely tonight, my dear."

That made her smile. "Thank you, Andrew. It's my new gown that makes me look so good. I like them. Much more than I thought I would. It was kind of you to buy them for me."

"It was nothing," he said, taking his own chair. "I'll buy you many more." He gazed at her speculatively. "So, you've had the afternoon to think. What will you have then? A diamond necklace? A ruby ring? A carriage of your own?" He laughed. "Or maybe a new horse—or two?"

She drew in a quick breath. She hadn't thought of any of those things. "No, Andrew. Though if I had to choose among those, I would take the horses."

He laughed again. "I know, my dear. I know *you*." He helped himself to some soup.

She moistened her lips. "Andrew?"

"Yes?"

"I—I have something to tell you."

He shrugged, his shoulders broad under his black evening coat. "Then tell me."

She took another breath. "You remember the child on the street? The one who rode Waterloo for me?"

He raised a dark eyebrow. "Yes? What about her?"

"I—" She must do this just right. She had to tell him the truth—she couldn't live with this thing untold between them. But she didn't want to spoil things. "I knew her already."

He paused, a spoonful of soup halfway to his mouth. "Knew her?" he repeated in surprise.

"Yes." Now that she'd begun she had to go on. "I—I buy flowers from her every morning after my ride. And—And I take her bread and meat."

Andrew put the soup in his mouth and swallowed slowly. Bridget waited anxiously. How could she convince him that she hadn't planned the whole thing? After the trick Papa had played on him about the race, would he believe anything she told him? But if she hadn't told him, and he found out later, that would have been even worse.

He looked her over, his eyes serious. Her breath caught in her throat, hung there while she waited.

And then he laughed. He put his soup spoon down on the tablecloth and laughed and laughed. "You set me up. And I fell right into it!"

"No, Andrew. Oh, no!" He couldn't believe that. "It wasn't like that at all. You chose the child."

He stopped laughing. "That's right." He scrutinized her face. "You mean that child had never been on the horse?"

"Never," Bridget said firmly. "I just bought her flowers and gave her food."

Andrew nodded. "I believe you, Bridget." He picked up his spoon again. "So I'll concede that you won the wager fair and square."

"Thank you." Relief swept through her. But there was still the payment of the bet. Would he still give her what she wanted?

"Well," he said, sending her a quizzical look. "What will you have?"

"I—I—" A big lump came up in her throat. "Please Andrew, let me tell you the whole thing before you speak."

He nodded over the rim of his glass, his gaze intent on her. "Go ahead. I'll listen."

She swallowed again, her throat dry. "I—the child—Elsie—has no parents. They're gone, dead. I—I want to take care of her, to bring her here. She could learn—And I—" She was rattling on. She closed her mouth with a snap.

"That's what you want?" he asked, his tone incredulous. "You want to bring a child—a child off the streets of London—*here?*"

"Yes," she said. "The people she lives with—the man drinks up all the money she earns. I worry about her out there in the streets. So little, so alone."

Andrew shook his head and her heart fell into her stomach. He was going to say no, to forbid her to ride in the park, to—

"Your heart is too tender," he pointed out. "You can't help every orphaned child in London."

"I know that," she replied, trying to keep the desperation out of her voice. "But I *can* help one, this one."

Andrew considered that, contemplating her thoughtfully. "You're right," he said finally.

She let out her breath. "You mean I can *have* her? I can bring her here?"

"Yes," he said. "You can. I promised you whatever you wanted. And I always keep my word."

She leaned toward him. "Oh, Andrew, thank you! I'll help Mrs. Purvey with her, I promise. And Elsie will be so good."

He laughed. "Bridget, children are always trouble. Don't make promises you can't keep."

She smiled then. "All right, but I'll do my best, at least."

He nodded. "There is one thing—one little thing."

She hesitated. "Yes?"

"About your morning rides."

Her heart fell. He couldn't ask her to give up her rides. She wasn't sure she could live without them. "Yes?"

"I can see why you like to ride so early." He paused, considering the tray the footman was presenting him. *"And* why you like to ride in breeches. But—"

She could hardly breathe. Why didn't he get on with it? Why didn't he tell her that her rides were over for good?

"But I ask that you continue to ride early. To be off the street before members of the *ton* are about."

She could hardly believe it. That was all he wanted? "Oh yes, I will!" she cried. "I'll be very careful, too. And I'll take Ned along. Always."

"Very good," Andrew said. "Then we'll consider it a

bargain. Tomorrow morning you can bring the child home with you. That should make you happy."

She swallowed over sudden tears. "Yes, Andrew, it does. Very happy. And thank you, thank you so much!"

The next morning Bridget was awake long before dawn. At the first streaks of daylight, she was off to the stable, and since she'd sent word the night before, Ned was ready.

"Do you think she'll want to come?" Bridget asked nervously as they moved along the still-quiet streets. "What if she's afraid?"

"She ain't gonna be afeerd," Ned said firmly. "Ye been real good to 'er."

"But—"

"Please, yer Ladyship. Don't be aworrying." Ned looked up at her from solemn eyes. "Anyone be glad to live at 'is Lordship's 'ouse. I knows."

Elsie wasn't on her corner yet, so they went on to the park. Bridget gave the stallion his usual run, but her heart wasn't in it. All she could think of was Elsie. Would she be there on her corner? Would she want to come?

The ride over, they headed back the way they'd come. As they neared the corner, Bridget's heart rose up in her throat. Elsie was there, the usual battered basket resting at her feet, full to the brim with fresh wildflowers.

Seeing Bridget, she smiled. "Morning, lady. I like that 'orse. 'E's nice."

Bridget smiled. "Yes, he is." She swung down, squatting so she could face the child on eye level. "Elsie, I have something important to say to you. Listen carefully."

"I listening, lady." The child's bright blue eyes were intent, unwavering.

"Yesterday, when you rode the horse, you did very well. His Lordship likes you. And—And we want you to come live with us."

"Live?" Elsie frowned. "Live?"

"Yes," Bridget said. "We want you to come to our house to stay. And you can have bread and meat every day."

"Every day?" Elsie's eyes grew bigger. "But, lady, what about me sister? Me Molly?"

Bridget swallowed. Why hadn't she thought about Molly?

"Well, she'll have more to eat if you're not there. And—And I'll send her bread and meat. Every day, I promise."

Elsie looked down at the basket by her bare feet. "Me flowers? What'll I do with me flowers?"

"Leave them," Bridget said.

"Oh no!" Elsie's little face wrinkled in horror. "Can't do that. Molly, Molly'll get beat. 'E'll beat 'er, 'e will."

Oblivious to the dirt, Bridget gathered the child to her. "Don't cry, Elsie. Please. We'll—We'll take your flowers to Molly's corner. And we'll tell her you're coming to live with us. So she won't worry about you."

Elsie wiped at her tear-stained face with grimy hands, leaving streaks in the dirt already there. "All right, lady."

They found Molly on her corner, a smaller edition of Elsie—complete with dirty face, bare feet, and grimy hands. She stared at Bridget from awe-struck eyes. "Yer Elsie's lady? The one what brings us the meat?"

Bridget nodded. "Now listen carefully. Elsie's coming to live with me."

Molly's face screwed up into tears. "She won't be coming 'ome with me?"

"No," Bridget said. "But there'll be more bread and meat for you." She swallowed hard. "And—And I'll see what I can do. Maybe you can come to the house, too."

"Me?" Molly was clearly amazed. "Me live with a lady?"

"Yes. You be a good girl now and I'll be back." How on earth was she going to talk Andrew into this?

She swung up on the horse and gave Elsie a hand up behind her. "Hold tight now."

As Elsie's little arms closed around her, Bridget heard a sob and looked back over her shoulder. Molly was standing, bravely holding out her flowers, but the tears were flowing down her cheeks. Bridget's own eyes filled with tears and she clucked to the horse.

By the time they'd reached the house, Elsie had stopped crying. Bridget went first to the kitchen to dispatch Ned with more bread and meat for Molly. Then she took Elsie to Mrs. Purvey. "This is the child I spoke to you about. Her name is Elsie."

Mrs. Purvey's round face broke into a delighted smile. "My, you're a pretty little thing," she said. "Come, we'll have you a bath first. And then I'll show you where to sleep."

Elsie stiffened. "I—I sleeps in the corner. With Molly. I ain't never slept by meself."

Mrs. Purvey extended a hand. "It'll be all right, child.

I'll have a cot put in with one of the maid's. You'll like it here."

Elsie's fingers clutched Bridget's so tightly she could hardly pry them loose. "You go with Mrs. Purvey, Elsie. And when you're all clean and in your new dress, she'll bring you to me."

"Dress?" Elsie asked, sniffling, but looking interested.

Mrs. Purvey nodded. "And shoes and stockings."

Elsie released her grasp on Bridget and put her little hand in Mrs. Purvey's. But she turned a worried face to Bridget. "Molly?" she said. "You won't forget me sister Molly?"

"I won't forget," Bridget said, conscious that Mrs. Purvey's smile had turned to a frown. She was worried, too, but she didn't want Elsie to see.

"You be good," she repeated. "And I'll see you later."

Chapter Eighteen

Two afternoons later Andrew entered White's and joined Peter at a table. "So," Peter said, "how is Aunt Sophie working out?"

Andrew sighed. "She and Bridget get along famously. Too famously, perhaps. But that's not the newest."

Peter took a sip of wine. "Tell me."

"Bridget made me another wager."

Peter grinned. "Don't tell me you lost it."

"I did," Andrew said. "She claimed that horse of hers doesn't like males."

Peter shook his head. "And you didn't believe her—so you lost the bet."

"Right."

Peter's eyes gleamed with devilment. "And that means?"

"She brought a waif off the street—a girl who sold flowers—to live at the house."

Peter's eyebrows shot up. "To live?"

Andrew nodded. "That's right. A wide-eyed little

waif." He sighed, trying to be fair. "She's a good enough child. Quiet. Well-behaved."

Peter took another sip of wine. "So?"

"So I just heard that there's a rumor going around."

Peter put his glass down. "I heard it, too."

Andrew frowned. "Why didn't you tell me?"

"I would have in a few minutes." Peter smiled. "Of course it may be a different rumor."

"God forbid!" Andrew cried. He dropped his head into his hands. "Tell me what you heard. And from whom."

"I heard it from Conigsby who had it from Drayton who had it from Linden who had it from Wichersham."

Andrew raised his head. "Wichersham!"

"Yes," Peter replied. "He said he had positive proof that this child is actually Bridget's bastard."

Andrew groaned. "Isn't that ridiculous! Bridget's only nineteen. The child's at least eight."

Peter put out a comforting hand. "Don't worry, old man. No one will believe it."

"Perhaps not," Andrew said. "But they will still talk—and talk. I tell you, Peter, this is driving me mad. If Bridget doesn't stop, I'll end up in Bedlam."

Peter chuckled. "You sound like a Cheltenham tragedy of the worst kind. The *ton* always talks: it has no other such enduring pastimes." He raised a quizzical eyebrow. "You never let it bother you before. Why now?"

Andrew contemplated his wineglass. "I'm not sure. Before Tom's death, when I wasn't the marquess, I didn't give a damn what they said about me. But now, somehow, it's different. Since my mother's gone—and I have Bridget—I don't want Bridget to be talked about, to suffer from all this gossip."

Peter traced a wine stain on the tablecloth with his fingertip. "I still think you're refining too much on the subject. You love Bridget. Don't be embarrassed. Yes, I know you love her." He laughed. "Everyone knows that."

Andrew straightened. "I'm certainly not embarrassed by loving her. Nor by Bridget's parentage." He frowned. "It's just that she doesn't behave properly and—"

Peter shrugged. "Properly? Who's to say what's proper?"

Andrew didn't smile. "You know very well that the *ton* says. So Peter, what do you suggest?"

"Well, if you must do something, do this. First, put Aunt Sophie to work whispering about Bridget's altruistic leanings—the true story might help there. Second, you might accompany your wife whenever she rides, and smile and look proud when she talks horses."

Andrew sighed. "I suppose I can do that. With some effort."

"And," Peter said, looking him straight in the eye, "when she races, you can be there to cheer her on."

Andrew groaned. "You expect me to cheer her on when she races in those godawful breeches?"

"Yes," Peter said with infuriating cheerfulness. "I do. What Bridget does isn't so unusual. The *ton's* had its female Jehus before, you know. We survived. So did they."

"Yes," Andrew said dryly. "Well, thank you for your advice."

Peter chuckled. "Advice you don't mean to follow."

Several afternoons later Bridget sat at her stitching. Aunt Sophie had gone calling—a tiresome task Bridget had gladly evaded. The fire screen she was needlepointing was beginning to look almost presentable. She was holding it off, admiring it, when Aunt Sophie came in.

"I am absolutely exhausted." Aunt Sophie sank into a chair, fanning herself with a limp hand. "This afternoon I have made some two dozen calls."

Bridget looked up from her yarn. "Two dozen? Aunt Sophie! Whatever are you making so many calls for?"

Aunt Sophie twisted her wedding ring and said nothing.

"Aunt Sophie?"

Aunt Sophie frowned. "Well, he didn't actually say not to tell you."

Bridget frowned, too, her stitching forgotten. "Who? Who is this *he?*"

"Andrew, of course. He sent me out to make these calls."

It all seemed very strange. "Whatever for?"

Aunt Sophie sighed. "Because the *ton* is talking about Elsie."

"Elsie? Why should they talk about her?"

Aunt Sophie avoided her gaze. "Actually, they're saying that she's yours."

"Mine?" Bridget repeated. "I don't understand."

"They're whispering about that you are Elsie's mother."

Bridget gasped. "Who started such a monstrous lie? And why didn't Andrew tell me?"

"I suppose," Aunt Sophie said, answering the last question first, "he didn't tell you because he knew you'd be upset."

Bridget swallowed. "He didn't—he didn't believe it, did he?"

"Of course not. That's why he sent me out to spread the true story about town."

Bridget stared. He couldn't have said—"You mean the *whole* story, that Andrew couldn't ride the horse? That he was thrown?"

"Yes," Aunt Sophie said, "the whole story. He felt that only the truth would quell the rumors."

"But Aunt Sophie, they will laugh at him. They'll laugh at Andrew."

Aunt Sophie shrugged. "I guess he didn't care about that. At least not as much as preserving your good reputation."

Bridget shuddered. "This is horrible. He's such a proud man. This will be degrading to him."

She leaped to her feet and began pacing the carpet. Suddenly she stopped and whirled. "Tell me, who was it? Who started this filthy rumor?"

Aunt Sophie patted her forehead with a lace-edged handkerchief. "We cannot be sure, of course. But the Lindens seem to be spreading it. And Wichersham."

Bridget cursed. "That bastard! He's always lying about me. Just because I wouldn't—I wouldn't let him—"

"Enough," Aunt Sophie said. "Every age has men like that." She straightened, arranging her skirt. "We can do little except evade them."

Bridget swore again. "If I were a man, I'd kill him. Or at least beat him to a bloody pulp!"

Aunt Sophie smiled complacently. "If he keeps this up, Andrew is apt to do that very thing."

* * *

The next morning Bridget awoke to find Andrew still beside her. He turned to her. "Shall we ride together today?"

"Yes," she said, smothering a little smile. She'd been hoping for this—hoping and praying.

The ride was uneventful, but as they turned back through the city, Bridget's heart rose up in her throat. "Andrew," she said, "there's something I'd like to show you."

"Very well."

He guided Sable after the stallion, stopping as she did in front of Molly. "I buy my nosegays from her now," she said.

Andrew nodded, reaching in his pocket for coins.

She forced herself to go on. "Andrew, this—this is Molly. Elsie's sister."

Andrew's eyebrows came together in a huge frown. "Bridget!"

"Flowers, milord?" Molly asked, her voice trembling. "Thank 'e, milord, fer helping me sister."

"You're welcome," Andrew said, obviously surprised. "Do you always work here?"

"Aye, milord. I sells me flowers. Every day 'ere, on me corner."

Bridget swallowed over the lump in her throat. "Please, Andrew. She's so little. And all alone."

"Bridget!"

Her heart pounded in her chest. He was very angry, but she had to go on. There were bruises on Molly's thin arms, bruises like those Mrs. Purvey had reported finding on Elsie's skinny body. She couldn't leave the child to be beaten. She just couldn't.

"Andrew, please, let me take her home. To her sister."

He scowled at her in utter disgust. "Bridget, be sensible. This city is full of orphans. You cannot possibly take them all in."

"I know, Andrew, I know. But Elsie has been very good. And Mrs. Purvey says it's all right." She swallowed. "If you let me take her, I will do whatever you say, promise whatever you ask."

He paused. "Whatever?"

She swallowed again. "Yes. If you wish, I won't ride in the mornings or——"

"No," Andrew said, "not that. You may ride." His face grew even more serious. "But if I let you take her, will you give up racing?"

Bridget looked down at the child whose great dark eyes were fastened on her in an agony of hope. It was a hard thing Andrew was asking her, to give up the excitement of the race. But she would have to do it. She couldn't leave Molly here.

Bridget looked into Andrew's eyes. "I'll give up racing," she said. "And I'll go further. If ever I race in public again, I—" She had to swallow over the hard words. "If ever I break my word and race again, I'll get out of your life forever. I promise."

"Agreed," Andrew said, extending his hand as he would to a man.

She shook it. Then she dismounted and drew near the child. "Molly, do you want to come home with me?"

The child nodded, tears trembling on her lashes. "Yes, milady, I does."

"Good." Bridget looked around. "Now, is there someone you can give your flowers to? You won't need them anymore."

Molly gulped. "Over there—the old woman. She be nice to me." She looked down at her bare feet. "Sometimes I shares my meat with 'er."

Bridget lifted the basket and, with Molly close beside her, carried it to the black-shawled old woman crouching in the corner of a doorway.

"Here," she said. "Molly's leaving these with you. She won't need them anymore."

The old woman raised her head, peering from watery eyes. "Yer the one, the one what took Elsie."

"Yes."

"And now yer taking 'er sister?"

"Yes."

"Praise the Lord! God bless, lady. God bless."

Bridget pressed a coin into her shaking hand and turned to the waiting child. "Come, Molly. We're going home."

Chapter Nineteen

Several weeks passed uneventfully. Bridget, engrossed in the little girls, spent most of her time helping Mrs. Purvey teach them. The girls, still incredulous about their good fortune, crept about the house like two clean and quiet little mice.

One afternoon Aunt Sophie came upon them while Bridget was industriously helping the girls practice their stitches. Hearing Aunt Sophie's chuckle, Bridget looked up.

"It's just that you present an amusing picture," Aunt Sophie said. "Short weeks ago you couldn't do a decent stitch. And now look at you!"

Bridget grinned. "Yes, I know. Look, I've fitted them each out with a basket, complete with design, needle, and yarn. They're learning fast, too." She chuckled. "I thought being a lady was dreadfully dull, but now that I have the girls I'm almost beginning to like it."

Aunt Sophie smiled. "You're an unusual lady, Bridget. Many ladies have little regard for those less fortunate than themselves. Would we had more who cared like you do."

Elsie raised her head, her face alight, her eyes shining. The needle poised in one tiny hand, she said, "She's an angel, our lady. A real angel."

Molly nodded, her little face screwed up intently. "She's good, she is. She give up racing 'er—*her* horse."

"Now, Molly," Bridget interrupted. She certainly didn't want that promise bruited about. The *ton* had enough to gossip about as it was. "That's—"

"But lady," the child hurried on and Bridget hadn't the heart to stop her. "You did promise." She looked toward her sister for confirmation and Elsie nodded. "I heard you, I did," Molly insisted. "You told 'im—*him*—that if you was bad and raced again you'd git outta his life."

Aunt Sophie sat down with a thud, her face turning white. "My word, Bridget! You actually promised Andrew that?"

Seeing the children staring at each other in fright, Bridget said softly, "Yes, I promised. But it wasn't that much, really it wasn't—I'm tired of racing anyhow." That wasn't true, of course, but she didn't want the girls to be upset by this talk. Their safety meant more than racing, even racing Waterloo.

She stopped Aunt Sophie's reply by turning immediately to the girls. "You've stitched enough for now. Run off to the kitchen and tell Cook to give you milk and cookies. And be sure to remember your manners."

Carefully the girls replaced their sewing in their individual baskets. Then they got to their feet and, hand in hand, decorously left for the kitchen.

Bridget felt her heart swelling with pride. "Aren't they just wonderful? They're learning so fast. You know, Aunt

Sophie, I like taking care of them. I think I'm going to be a good mother."

Aunt Sophie came erect, putting a hand to her startled mouth. "Bridget! You're not already—"

Bridget laughed. "No, no, Aunt Sophie. Of course not." She smiled happily. "But when I am, I shall not mind it. Not in the least."

Aunt Sophie settled back in her chair with a sigh of relief. "Thank goodness you're not *enceinte* now. I simply couldn't cope with that at present." She twisted her wedding ring. "You know, Bridget dear, I've been meaning to tell you. You're doing very well in learning the ways of the *ton*. Why, last week when Lady Jersey came to call, you were the pattern card of perfection. You never mentioned horses to her at all."

"I'm trying hard," Bridget said. And she was. But from the look on Aunt Sophie's face, maybe she wasn't trying hard enough. Why did the *ton* have to be so particular about things? She sighed. "All right, you might as well tell me. I can see it from your expression that I'm still doing something wrong."

Aunt Sophie sighed, twisting the ring some more. "It's not exactly *wrong*, dear," she said rather sadly. "It's just—well—the way you're raising the girls."

"What's wrong with the way I'm raising the girls?" Bridget asked. If she was doing something wrong, she wanted to know. She wouldn't for the world hurt those precious little girls.

"You're raising them like ladies," Aunt Sophie said. "And they are not."

"I'm helping them improve themselves," Bridget said. "Surely no harm can come of that."

183

Aunt Sophie sighed deeply. "But it can. Think, my dear. You're giving them false expectations. They cannot hope to marry well." She frowned. "They have no dowries. And so unless they're great beauties, they will be passed over in the marriage mart. If that happens, they'll be fortunate to snag a tradesman. And if they're not successful there, they'll marry a poor man—or end up back on the streets."

"Never!" Bridget cried. "I won't let that happen to them." The thought of either of them having to sell flowers again put a cold chill through her. And Aunt Sophie wasn't just talking about selling flowers. She was talking about something far worse, something Bridget couldn't even bear to consider.

"You won't be able to prevent it," Aunt Sophie pointed out unhappily. "You have no power, no funds. Too bad your father couldn't settle a dowry on you. Something of your own."

"But he did," Bridget replied. "He gave me Waterloo."

"Hardly a proper dowry," Aunt Sophie said with a sad little smile. "But never mind. Perhaps I'm refining over much on the subject. They are both safe for now. That should be enough."

They went back to their stitching then, letting the subject drop, but Bridget's mind would give her no rest, presenting her with one horrifying picture after another— the girls hungry and cold, huddled in a doorway, beaten by angry men, trampled by carriage horses. A hundred horrible possibilities followed one another through her mind in terrifying progression.

Her fingers went on steadily stitching, but her heart was cold. Something had to be done. And it had to be done right away. She would not be able to sleep until she was assured of the girls' safety.

The Lindens' carriage pulled up at the house at the same time as Andrew's. Too late he recognized it—too late to keep on, too late to run away, too late to do anything but pin a false smile on his face and try to look pleased to see the last people on the earth he wanted to see. He knew his smile would not convince anyone who knew him, but he did his best, determined not to give these prattling talebearers any more ammunition in their war against Bridget.

"Lord Haverly," Lady Linden gushed, swinging around to face him and almost decapitating her daughter with her huge hat in the process. "How wonderful to see you! I was hoping you'd be at home."

At least she didn't know what he was thinking—that he wished he were *not* at home, wished it devoutly.

He sighed. Today she was wearing a greenish-yellow monstrosity, in a particularly bilious shade that reminded him a great deal of pond slime. Obviously the woman needed a new dressmaker, someone with some sense of style and color.

"Good day," he said. Good breeding insisted that he work hard at being pleasant. "Come to visit Bridget, have you?"

"Oh yes, Lord Haverly." This time it was the daughter who was gushing. Did these two never say anything in a normal tone of voice?

"Come in," he said, the lie sticking between his teeth. "Bridget will be glad to see you."

Inside, he waited while Purvey took their bonnets. Then he led their guests into the sitting room.

Bridget looked up from the little girls, a smile on her face when she spied him, the smile fading when she glimpsed their visitors behind him.

"Look who's here," he said, trying to sound cheerful. "The Lindens have come to call on us."

Bridget remained silent, reaching out to draw the little girls protectively close. He saw the flicker of apprehension in her eyes.

The girls, in turn, stood timidly staring at the monstrous bulk in front of them, their faces wreathed in amazement at such a sight.

"Good day, Lady Linden. Martine." Aunt Sophie rose from a chair near the hearth and graciously approached the visitors. "Sorry we haven't returned your call yet. We've been rather busy with Bridget's newest altruistic endeavor. Such sweet little girls."

"Yes, indeed." Lady Linden's eyes gleamed with avid curiosity. She fastened her gaze on the little girls, who shrank back against Bridget. "Blond, the both of them," Lady Linden said, shifting her gaze pointedly to Bridget's auburn curls.

When Bridget didn't answer but drew the girls closer still, Aunt Sophie spoke again. "They're very good girls. Bridget has done wonders with them."

"Like a regular little mother," Lady Linden observed, in a tone that conveyed much more than the words.

Andrew restrained himself, but he wanted to shove his fist down the prattler's throat, to hit her over the head with a blunt object. Anything to shut her big red mouth and wipe that look of growing aversion off his wife's pale face.

Aunt Sophie sent him a calming look; probably she could tell how close he was to erupting in outraged anger. "Yes," she said calmly, soothingly. "Bridget will make an excellent mother—when she is ready to begin her family."

Martine paused in her circuit of the room. She set down the Sèvres shepherdess she was examining and snickered, but before she could make any comment, Bridget smiled lovingly at the little girls. "Mrs. Purvey will be waiting for you. Go now for your lessons."

"Yes, lady," the little girls chorused. Thank God, Andrew thought, that she hadn't encouraged them to call her Mother! What the Lindens would make of that!

He watched them go, watched Bridget turn back to the visitors, a patently false smile on her face. "I hear that Farrington's Folly has a learned pig," she said, in an obvious effort to change the topic of conversation.

Martine put down a fragile vase with a thud that made him wince and almost reach out to rescue the *objet* from destruction. "Yes," she said, with a superior smirk. "I've seen it. It's nothing special. There's a trick to it, of course."

One look at Bridget's face told him she was near losing all patience. And no wonder. His own patience was fading fast. "What is the trick?" he inquired, rather more sharply than he wished. "Explain it to me."

Martine pursed her thin mouth in disgust. "How should I know what the trick is? I just know no animal can be that smart. It's just ridiculous to think they can function like humans."

187

That did it. He saw Bridget's mouth opening. He was surprised she'd contained herself this long. "Animals are very intelligent," she insisted. "And if it is a trick, well, the pig has to be smart to learn it. Horses are very intelligent. I know that."

Martine snickered even louder. "Horses again. With you it's always horses."

Bridget straightened, her mouth firming into a grim line. "Yes, horses."

Lady Linden smiled, a smile so false it practically curdled his blood. "I hear that you are a great racer," she said to Bridget.

"Oh yes, I like to race," Bridget replied. "Feeling the wind in your face and a swift horse between—"

"Yes," Andrew interrupted hastily. "But you can get the same effect with a good fast gallop."

"Not exactly," Bridget said. "In a gallop there's no competition. Competition heightens it."

"It must be most exciting," Lady Linden cooed, clapping her hands gleefully. "Why, I know several people who've said they'd love to race you and your wonderful Waterloo."

He held his breath. How would Bridget respond to this, this almost dare on Lady Linden's part? Should he interfere?

He decided in favor of keeping his mouth shut. Bridget had made a promise. And he would trust her to keep it.

She shrugged eloquently. "Racing is fun, but I no longer race. I—"

"No longer!" Lady Linden cried, clasping her hands to her ample breast in exaggerated dismay. "Oh, Lord Wichersham will be most disappointed."

"Wichersham?" Bridget repeated, her voice rising. *"He* wants a race with me?"

"Indeed yes," Lady Linden continued. "Why, the man can speak of nothing else."

It was time to interfere, Andrew judged, before Bridget forgot she was a lady and said something she shouldn't. "Speaking of horses," he said, pulling out his watch and glancing at it, nonchalantly he hoped, "surely, Bridget, you haven't forgotten that we've promised to meet Peter for a ride in Hyde Park? And the hour is rapidly approaching."

He looked at her, hoping by a warning wink to keep her from starting in surprise at news of this appointment he'd just made up. He was grateful to see realization dawning on her face. "Oh yes," she cried, almost gaily, glancing at the mantel clock with a smile. "We don't want to keep Peter waiting. He loves our rides so."

"Then you'd best run along and change into your habit," Aunt Sophie said, getting into the game with her best smile. "I'm sure our guests won't mind."

"Of course not," Lady Linden agreed, turning her bulk toward the clock. "My, it is late. Later than I thought. Martine and I must be going, too. So many calls to make. And so little time."

Of course, he thought, she'd gotten what she'd come for. More gossip to carry about the city.

When she hoisted her bulk to her feet, Bridget rose, too, sending him a half-anxious glance.

"Go along and change," he told her. "I'll just see our guests out."

* * *

It wasn't till bedtime that Bridget had the opportunity to speak to Andrew. When he opened the door from his room and came in wearing his dressing gown, he was smiling. "Well, we've survived another visit from the Lindens. And you handled yourself very well."

She managed a rueful smile. "You know that I wouldn't have received them if they'd come a little earlier—or a little later. Not with you. To tell you the truth, I don't know why anyone speaks to them at all. They're such terrible people."

"I know," he said, pulling her into his arms. "But it's over now."

Of course he would say that, not mentioning that they would be back. People like them were always out there, ready to harm the girls. "Andrew?"

"Yes, my love?"

She leaned against his chest, relishing his closeness. There was such comfort in his arms. "I want to ask you something."

He dropped a kiss on her neck. "Then ask away," he said, running a trail of more kisses down to her shoulder. "What is it?"

She took a deep breath. "I'm worried about the girls."

He drew back, looking down at her from dark troubled eyes. "They look fine to me. Just fine."

"I know, but we were talking earlier today, Aunt Sophie and I. And she said some things about what will happen to the girls when they grow up. They have no family, no portions, no dowries. If something happens to us, they won't be safe. And that troubles me greatly."

She heard Andrew's deep deep sigh. "You want me to give them dowries, is that it?"

"Would you?" she asked, daring to raise her gaze to his. "Would you do that for me? It would relieve my mind no end."

He was frowning fiercely, and she held her breath, waiting for him to tell her he wouldn't do it, that he had reached the end of his patience about these girls.

She couldn't really blame him. He'd been most generous.

She would have to think of something else, find some other way to help them. She had very little money. What else was there that was her own? Nothing but Waterloo. She couldn't give him up, but the girls—

She swallowed over the lump in her throat. "You said, you said that Waterloo was mine. I'll give him—to you. If—" She had to try twice to get the words out over the great lump. "If—If you—have to—sell him—to get enough—"

Andrew held her off at arm's length, his expression incredulous. "My God, Bridget, stop it!" He shook her lightly. "You should know I'd never sell your horse! The horse you love!" He pulled her to him. "What kind of monster do you think I am? If the girls mean that much to you, I'll see to it that they're taken care of. I promise you." He smoothed her hair, dropped a kiss on her forehead. "I'll go tomorrow to my solicitor—and have a trust set up for them."

"And guardians?" Bridget asked anxiously. "I have to be sure they're really safe."

"Yes," he said, "guardians, too. Aunt Sophie and Peter both. Will that set your heart at rest?"

She reached up to kiss him soundly. "Yes, Andrew, it will. Thank you. You're a good man. Very good to me. I love you, you know." And she proceeded to show him how much.

Chapter Twenty

The days passed, bright beautiful summer days that Andrew enjoyed like he'd enjoyed no others he could remember. And one August afternoon he met Peter at White's.

"There he is," Peter said, looking up with that devilish smile of his. "The man who lives in Lady Haverly's pocket. Or so all London whispers."

"So that's what they're saying." Andrew grinned. "I don't really care." He opened his arms wide, so happy he wanted to embrace the whole world. "Look at me, Peter, just look at me!"

Peter whistled speculatively. "I'm looking. What am I supposed to see?"

Laughing, Andrew settled into his chair. "You see before you the happiest man in all London."

Peter raised an eyebrow. "Indeed! If my memory serves me right, you used to be the most notorious man in all London. Busy with this lady and that, this not-lady and that. And now—now you're the most besotted of men." He grinned again. "Besotted, of all things, with your own wife! So, tell me, what has occasioned this marvelous transformation?"

"You know," Andrew said, conscious that he was grinning foolishly. "It's Bridget. I have a beautiful wife—the most beautiful woman in all London."

"You're right about that," Peter said. "I've always believed her beautiful." He raised the other eyebrow. "Your marriage appears to be flourishing. And I take it the little girls are behaving themselves well."

Andrew smiled. "I can't believe I made such a fuss about her taking them in. They're sweet little things." He laughed sheepishly. "You don't know what it's like, my friend, to have two little girls hanging on your every word, looking at you adoringly like you were—were—"

"God?" Peter inquired devilishly. "You forget, I've been there at the house with you. I've seen them adoring you. Yes, I think God fills the bill."

Still feeling foolish, Andrew laughed again. "Well, almost. But seriously, my friend, fatherhood is beginning to look to me like a rather interesting business." He sighed expansively. "You know, I believe I shall actually enjoy it."

Peter nodded. "Well, it certainly sounds like life is treating you well."

"It is," Andrew said. "Very well. And Bridget has even kept her promise."

"What promise is that?" Peter inquired innocently, helping himself to some more wine.

Andrew extended his glass to be filled. "Oh yes, I didn't tell you. When we took in the second child, she promised me she would never race again. And she has kept her promise. Kept it admirably. Oh yes," he repeated. "I am a fortunate man. Life could not be better."

Pouring his wine, Peter frowned. "I hesitate to say this to a man in your obvious state of euphoria, my friend, but when life cannot be better, you'd best beware. It inevitably gets worse."

Andrew sipped slowly, refusing to feel concern. "Come now, Peter, you're getting to be a crotchety old man afraid of the dark. Bridget loves me. I love her. What could go wrong?"

Andrew recalled their conversation the next afternoon when the letter arrived from his steward in Scotland. He didn't want to leave Bridget—actually he hated to leave her, to be away from her at all, but from the tone of McFarland's letter his presence there at the estate was just about a necessity.

So, sighing, he went to find his wife. Mrs. Purvey told him she was in the sitting room with the little girls, directing their stitching. He watched them from the doorway for a moment—the very picture of familial bliss. Perhaps one day before too long there would be a babe in a cradle. His babe.

"Busy, are you?" he asked cheerfully. All three of them looked up, smiling when they saw him.

"Andrew," Bridget cried happily. "Come in. We're stitching again. The girls are doing so much better." She shifted her gaze to the letter in his hand. "Have you news there?"

Andrew nodded. "Yes, from McFarland. I told you about him—my steward in Scotland. I'm afraid it's not particularly good news either. There's some kind of problem and he writes that he needs me there."

Her smile slowly faded. But his heart lifted to see it—this physical indication that she didn't want him to go away, even for few days. "Does that mean you must go?" she asked.

"I'm afraid so." He paused. "Why don't you come along with me?"

Her growing smile made his heart beat faster. "To Scotland, you mean?"

"Yes, you know I hate to be away from you."

He could almost see her thinking, considering all the ramifications of going with him. She glanced down at the girls. "But if I go, what about them? Can they come along?"

Andrew frowned. Much as he wanted her with him, he had to tell her the truth. "It's a long journey, Bridget. And it's hard on children—even good children like these," he smiled at the girls, "to be cooped up in a carriage for hours on end like that."

When the little girls moved closer to her, as though fearing her departure, Bridget sighed. "I'd like to go with you, Andrew, but I suppose I'd better not. It wouldn't be good to leave them so soon."

She looked so forlorn he couldn't bear it, so he hurried to reassure her. "It'll be all right," he said. "I'll make it as fast as I can. I shouldn't be away more than a week. While I'm gone, you can make plans to finish redecorating your bedchamber."

Bridget nodded. "That's true. So many things keep interfering that I've hardly had time to look at materials.

Yes, that's what I'll do. When you get back, we'll have all our choices made."

The first two days that Andrew was gone passed so slowly that Bridget thought each one as long as a year. It was dreadful the way she missed him. But she spent even more time with the girls. There was so much to teach them. So much they needed to learn.

And she engaged them and Peggy in the enjoyable task of viewing fabric swatches for the new bedroom furnishings. Though it was fun, it was hard to keep her mind on redecorating. She kept wanting Andrew—to hear his voice, to see his smile, to touch his hand.

The second afternoon, she was closeted with the girls, discussing bed hangings, when Purvey appeared in the doorway, his usually bland face perturbed. "A man, your Ladyship, an Irishman. He says he's your father."

"Papa?" Bridget got to her feet. She'd been neglecting him shamefully since the girls came; she hadn't been out to the stables for days. Was that what had brought him here? "Show him in," she said.

When Purvey left, barely keeping himself from shaking his head, she turned to the little girls. "You're going to meet my papa. Remember I told you about him?"

Elsie nodded, but her eyes looked worried. "You said he's nice. He don't—he doesn't beat you."

"That's right," Bridget said. "You mustn't be afraid of him." She gave them each a hug. "He talks loud, but he won't hurt you."

"All right, lady," Molly said, "if you says so."

When Papa came in, his face looking worried, Bridget left the girls and went to hug him. "Papa! It's so good to see you! I'm sorry I haven't been out to the stables lately. I've been terribly busy with the girls."

He returned her hug. "Never mind that, Bridget, me girl. I understand. So, these here are the little ones ye sent word about." He looked down at the girls who had come to hang onto her skirts.

"Yes, Papa. This is Elsie and this is Molly. Aren't they wonderful?"

"Wonderful," Papa repeated, smiling down at them. "And pretty, too." The girls smiled at that—and when he reached in his pocket and pulled out two pennies, pressing one into each of their hands, they actually giggled. Then he turned to her. "Bridget, girl, I need to talk to ye. Alone, if ye please."

When he looked like that—his eyes so worried, his face all wrinkled up in a great frown—it was serious. "Of course, Papa." She turned to the girls. "Elsie, Molly, why don't you go out to the kitchen to Mrs. Purvey? I think it was about now she was going to teach you about making bread."

"Yes, lady."

She watched them go, shut the door softly behind them, and turned anxiously to him. "All right, Papa. Tell me what it is. Is there something I can do to help you?"

Papa pulled his pipe from his pocket. "Kin I smoke in here? Will Andrew mind?"

"Of course not." She swallowed. She didn't like the sound of this. Something must be terribly wrong. "Sit down, Papa."

He shook his head. "Thanks no, girl. I think better on me feet." He filled his pipe, tamping it firmly. " 'Tis a hard thing I've come to tell ye, a real hard thing. And ye see, I just don't know how to go on about it."

And then it struck her! Her heart pounded in her throat. Her hands went all sweaty. "Andrew! Dear God, something has happened to Andrew!" Shaking, she reached out. "Papa, please, what is it? Tell me!"

"No, no!" He grabbed her by the shoulders, steadying her. "Bridget, girl, stop it now! 'Tis nothing about Andrew I've come to tell ye. I haven't seen Andrew these many days. This thing—'Tis about me."

The breath left her lungs in a great whoosh of relief. "Papa, please! Whatever it is, then, just tell me! Tell me now."

He lit his pipe, puffing till it was going well. "I'll tell ye, girl, but 'tis shamed I am by it. Real shamed."

She sank into a chair, pleating her hands together anxiously in her lap. "Papa, no matter what you've done, you know I love you."

He sighed. "I know, girl. I know. 'Tis a longish story, so bear with me while I tell it."

"Yes, Papa." She tried to lean back in the chair, tried to look patient.

"I got to go back some, to before the race." He clutched his pipe. "Wichersham came out to the stables. You 'member the day?"

She nodded. "Yes. I was working a colt. I heard you yell, 'No,' but that was all I could hear."

Papa scowled. "He made me that angry, the rotter! He had me IOUs. Lots of—"

She stared up at him. "So he was the one! Andrew told me he paid your debts, but he didn't say it was to Wichersham."

"Aye," Papa said. "Wichersham bought up me vowels." He swallowed. "Andrew told me ye knew 'bout the IOUs, but not who bought them." He sighed. "Well, it were like this—he had me vowels and he said he'd take the stallion in exchange."

"Waterloo?" She thought she would faint away. "Papa, you couldn't! You couldn't give Waterloo to that horrible man!"

Papa nodded. "Course I couldn't! I know ye love that animal—more 'an life itself, I'm thinking."

She swallowed, trying to get calm. There must be more, else why was Papa there? "Papa, what else did Wichersham say to you that day?"

He avoided her gaze. "I didn't want to tell ye. I couldn't. The bounder—he wanted the stallion—or—or—" He puffed furiously.

She kept her gaze on him, waiting, her breath coming in shallow gasps. "Or what? Go on, Papa. Tell me all of it."

"He wanted *ye*," Papa cried, his face gone scarlet. "He said he'd take ye instead of the blunt. Make ye his—his—oh Lord, girl, I can't say it!"

"Oh, Papa!" Leaping to her feet, she hurried to his side. "Oh, that horrible man! How could he?"

Papa's scowl got fiercer. "He ain't got no heart, that's how. Ye can always tell a bad 'un from the way he treats his stock. And you know how bad he were to *them*." He frowned. "I'd of gone to prison, but I had to think about ye. I couldn't be sure what'd happen to ye—and the horse."

Bridget backed off. That explained the whole curious thing. "Papa! The race!"

"Aye," he said, his face reddening even more in embarrassment. "That race with Sable, it were fixed."

"Fixed!" She could hardly believe her ears. Her own father doing such a terrible thing. "Papa, how could you?"

"I had to save ye," he said stubbornly. "The both of ye. And that were the only thing I could think of."

"So you set up the race—and the wager," she said, still hardly believing it.

"Aye."

She stared at him—her own father cheating. "I wondered why Waterloo lost that race. I couldn't understand it."

" 'Twas all I could think of to do. I knew his Lordship," Papa went on. "He'd been coming out there long enough fer me to trust him. I knew he'd do right by ye."

She took a deep breath. As always, Papa had done his best for her. "And he has," she said. "It's all right, Papa. We're both safe."

"Aye." Papa sighed deeply. "I thought so at the time. I thought I done right. But it weren't enough. Ye ain't safe."

Her heart began to pound again. Oh no! This sounded even more frightening. "Oh, Papa, now what?"

"Wichersham, what else?" Papa cried, letting go with a string of curses that burned her ears. "He's got his hands on some more of me notes."

"Papa!"

He frowned at her. "Don't be looking at me that way. It ain't like that, girl. I don't wager no more. He bought up me bills from the tradesmen. Business's been slow lately, and I got behind on me payments. And now he's got me bills."

Maybe business had fallen off because she was no longer there, but Papa didn't want to say it. "What does he want this time?" she asked contritely.

Papa looked puzzled. "That's the peculiar thing 'bout it all. He says he just wants a race—'tween Waterloo and his horse. He says he'll consider me notes paid no matter who wins. So I come to ask you to race fer me."

Bridget's heart tried to climb out of her mouth. Wichersham knew! He must have known about her promise to Andrew not to race. But how? Who could have told him? Only the two of them knew—and the girls and Aunt Sophie. But they wouldn't be talking to Wichersham.

She swallowed. She had to tell Papa something. "But, Papa, I don't race anymore. It's—It's not ladylike."

Papa smiled faintly. "I know ye ain't raced lately," he said. "But knowing how ye love it, I thought ye might be willing. And to be truthful, Bridget, me girl, I ain't wanting to go to prison." He frowned. "But I couldn't bring meself to ask Andrew fer blunt agin."

"You couldn't anyway," she said quickly. "Andrew's away in Scotland. Though, if he were here, I'd ask him myself." She tried to think. She couldn't let Papa go to prison, but if she raced, if she broke her promise . . . She had to have time to think.

"Listen, Papa, when does Wichersham want this race?"

"Three days hence," Papa said. "At the stables."

She led him toward the door. "Give me a little time to think about it, Papa. We'll work it out. I'll send word to Andrew right away."

"Aye," Papa said, enveloping her in a quick hug. "I

knew ye'd be there fer me. I'll be by tomorrow then. Thank 'ee, Bridget. Ye're a good girl. Yer Mama'd be that proud of ye."

As soon as Papa left, Bridget hurried off to find Aunt Sophie. Fortunately she had just returned from making afternoon calls and was still in the foyer, removing her newest bonnet.

"Aunt Sophie," Bridget said, trying to remain calm. "Would you please come into the sitting room? I need to speak to you."

"Of course. I'll be right there."

Aunt Sophie followed her down the hall, closing the door behind them. "All right, Bridget, what's wrong? Have the Lindens been calling again?"

"The Lindens?" For a minute she couldn't think. "No, no. Papa was here and the most horrible thing has happened."

"Tell me," Aunt Sophie said, settling on the sofa beside her. "What has happened?"

Bridget swallowed. "You'll have to know the whole story. It starts before Andrew and I were married." And she told Aunt Sophie the whole sordid tale, ending with, "So that is how Andrew and I happened to wed. But now you see, I love him. And if I race, if I break my promise, I will be duty-bound to leave him." She blinked, trying in vain to hold back the tears.

Aunt Sophie pressed a handkerchief into her hands. "But if you don't race?"

"Then Papa will go to debtor's prison. And how can I let that happen? He could have—" She swallowed. "Papa could have told me what Wichersham offered before.

And—And I would have done it. For him I would have done it!"

She shuddered. "To save Papa I would have let that vile man set me up in keeping! And oh, Aunt Sophie, I think it would have killed me!"

"Now, now," Aunt Sophie said, patting her hand. "That didn't happen—and it won't. You're quite safe from Wichersham." She frowned. "But your father . . ."

"Aunt Sophie, what will I do?"

Aunt Sophie frowned. "First, we send word to Andrew. Surely when he knows the circumstances, he will understand."

Bridget sighed. "I don't think so. There were to be no exceptions. Do you think he might get back in time to pay the notes? And I won't have to race?"

Aunt Sophie looked doubtful. "It takes time—the trip from Scotland. And he's not due back till next week. But we'll send anyway."

She rang for Purvey and when he appeared, she said, "Send word to the stable. We want the fastest horse—not Waterloo—and a light rider."

"Ned!" Bridget cried. "We'll send Ned."

"Yes," Aunt Sophie agreed. "Provisions for the first leg of the journey—and funds for the rest."

Purvey nodded and left.

"Paper and pen," Aunt Sophie said, hurrying to the desk. "You must write it all out for him."

Ten minutes later, Ned appeared in the doorway, cap in hand. "Yer Ladyship," he said, his voice tentative. "They said ye'd be wanting me?"

"Yes," Bridget said, jumping up from the desk. "I'm sending you to Scotland with a message to his Lordship.

It's important, Ned, very important. Don't waste any time, but have a care for your horse."

She pressed the bag Purvey had brought minutes before into his hands. "There's food in here, and here are some coins for later in the journey. And this is the letter."

He tucked the missive inside his shirt. "I'll keep it safe, yer Ladyship. And don't ye worry none. I'll find him—he'll be home soon."

"Thank you, Ned. Godspeed."

She watched him out the door. "If anyone can reach him in time, it's Ned. I pray God he can do it."

Chapter Twenty-one

The next day when Papa came round again, Bridget told him not to worry. If Andrew didn't get back in time, she would ride in the race. Papa went off content, and she turned to the girls, though she found it almost impossible to concentrate on the materials they were examining.

But Papa hadn't been gone long before Purvey appeared in the doorway again, this time his face clearly twisted in distaste. "Another caller, milady. Lord Wichersham."

"Wichersham! Now what—" She didn't want to see him. "Tell him I'm not—" She stopped herself. Maybe she could reason with the man. "Wait, I've changed my mind. Show him in, Purvey. And—And then wait outside the door, out of sight but within hearing. Only come in if I call for you."

Purvey looked surprised, but he replied, "Yes, milady."

After Bridget sent the girls to the kitchen, she got to her feet, straightening her skirt and her countenance at the same time. She would stay calm, not let Wichersham provoke her. What could the man want here? Did he want just to crow over her? Or was it something else?

He came sauntering in, his expensive clothes looking as ill fitting as usual. "Lady Haverly," he said, his voice a raspy sneer. "Or should I say, my dear Bridget. Good afternoon."

Her name on his lips raised the fine hairs on the back of her neck. She didn't want to bother with the amenities, but it was better not to aggravate the man. "Good afternoon." She could hear the hint of fear in her voice. All she could do was hope Wichersham couldn't. "What brings you here?" she asked.

"You." He let his gaze travel down over her body, then slowly up again, letting it linger on her bosom till she felt the color flood her cheeks.

"What do you mean?"

"I mean your father foiled me before—when I would have taken *you* in lieu of his notes."

She clamped her teeth together firmly. It was embarrassing that Purvey was hearing all this, but she had to have him close by. How could she have dreamed she would have let this awful man touch her? She'd never have been able to stand it.

When she didn't answer, Wichersham went on, his voice a harsh obscene caress. "And now, my dear, I have another chance."

She shook her head. "I don't know what you're talking about. You have no chance with me. You never had."

He seemed not even to have heard her. "I know your father told you about my first offer." His little eyes gleamed with rancor. "And I know about your promise to your husband not to race."

"How?" she stammered. "How did you find out?"

He smiled, a loathsome smile that made her blood freeze in her veins. "I have my ways. And my ears. The Lindens, for example."

"But I didn't tell them," Bridget said numbly, wishing this awful nightmare was over. "I didn't tell anyone."

"It doesn't matter," Wichersham replied, smoothing his hair with a gloved hand. "What matters is that I *do* know. And I also know that if you race, you lose your husband. That makes it all much sweeter." He scowled. "I've been waiting for this. A score to settle with him. He paid up Varley's vowels, you know. Spoiled my fun."

Fun? What was he talking about? "Why should you want to send Peter to prison? Or Papa either? I don't understand."

"I like power," he said. "And I like using it."

And she saw, incredibly, that he meant it. He actually enjoyed hurting people.

When he took a step closer, she held her ground, grateful that Purvey was out there. But even so, she wasn't going to let Wichersham get any closer.

She swallowed hastily. "I'll pay my father's bills. How much does he owe?"

Wichersham laughed, a cold caustic sound with no humor in it. "I'm not accepting payment from you. Or anyone else. I insist on the race."

Bridget twisted her hands into her skirt. "If you wait till Andrew returns, he'll pay you double the notes' value." She knew before she spoke that it was futile, but she had to try.

He laughed again, raising goose bumps on her bare arms. How could the man be so barbarous? Why did he want to hurt her?

"Why?" she cried. "Why are you doing this to me?"

Wichersham shrugged, his expression bland and yet somehow evil. "It's simple enough. I want you. And I get what I want. Come," he said smoothly, "be reasonable. I don't ask for so much. One night with me. Or even an afternoon. And I'll forget the race—and your father's bills."

He took a step toward her, his gloved hand outstretched.

"No!" she cried. "I would never do such a thing! Never!"

He shrugged nonchalantly. "Have it your own way, my dear. But think about it. A few hours—and Haverly need never know." He leered. "I promise you an enjoyable time."

"I would die first," Bridget said, her hands clenching into fists she no longer bothered to hide. If he touched her, she would hit him—hit him and scream. "Now get out of here before I call for someone to *help* you out."

"Very well. But mark my words. You'll be sorry. I'll see to it. Oh yes, I'll see to it."

After he left, Bridget went back to the girls, trying to keep herself busy, so busy that at night she could fall exhausted into the bed she had shared with Andrew.

But no matter how long or how hard she worked, sleep seemed forever in coming. The great bed was big and cold and empty. And lying there in the darkness, her cheeks wet with tears, she wondered if ever again she would share it with the man she loved.

She tried to figure out where she could go, how she could provide for the girls. But the only thing she could think of was to take them to Papa's, to raise them at the stables. Papa would let her do that—she knew he would.

She even thought of telling Papa the truth, telling him about her promise. If he knew, he wouldn't let her race, but then he would go to prison. And she couldn't bear that. Not after he'd done so much for her.

Tossing and turning till the bed was one great tangle of sheets and covers, she tried to think of some other way to help Papa, some way that wouldn't mean breaking her promise to Andrew, wouldn't mean losing him. She loved him so much. But there was no other way. Papa had to be saved.

Wichersham had said he was doing this on purpose. He was determined to ruin her marriage. Of course, Papa had played right into his hands by falling behind on his bills, but even if he hadn't, Wichersham would have looked for some other way to hurt them. As it was, he had them in a trap—there was no escape.

Their only hope was if Andrew returned in time. If she could see him face to face, talk to him before she raced, surely she could convince him to let her ride. Or maybe he could make Wichersham take payment for the notes. Andrew could be very forceful. Even Wichersham would give way before him.

She prayed that Andrew would return in time. She prayed and she waited. But the days passed—and the long nights, too—and Andrew didn't come home.

The day of the race dawned dark and dreary, like her spirit, Bridget thought, but by afternoon the weather was better. There would be no rain to cancel the race.

Feeling like she was going to her own execution, she

joined Aunt Sophie and the girls in the carriage. Waterloo would follow sedately behind, a groom sitting in the back to watch over him.

Bridget had intended to leave the girls at home with Mrs. Purvey, so she was surprised to see them dressed and already in the carriage.

"Aunt Sophie, I don't know—"

"They should be there," Aunt Sophie insisted. "After all, it's their future, too." She forced a smile. "Don't look so worried, my dear. All will be well. Andrew loves you. I'm sure of it."

Bridget wanted to believe that, but she wasn't nearly as sure as Aunt Sophie. True, Andrew had been good to her. But he had never *said* he loved her. And the circumstances of their marriage had been so odd.

No, she couldn't count on love on his part. Andrew was very particular about doing the "proper" thing—and when he found she'd raced, that she'd broken her promise, he would hold her to her word. He would expect her to do as she'd promised—and get out of his life.

The stable yard was crowded with people, fashionable lords and their ladies all out for an exciting afternoon. Blacklegs, too, ready to take bets. "Look at this," Aunt Sophie said in disgust. "Everyone is here. Wichersham must have talked the race all round London."

Peering out the window, Bridget nodded. "There's a terrible crush out there. An awful crowd. Be sure the girls don't get lost in it."

"Bridget," Aunt Sophie said. "Please! Give off worrying about these girls. I'll hold tightly to their hands. I promise you, they'll never leave my side."

Bridget knew she was too anxious to make much sense.

"Thank you, Aunt Sophie. I've got to go get ready." She looked down at the girls, managing a smile for their sakes. She kissed them each on the cheek, got a hug from each. "You be good girls now. I'll see you when the race is over."

She climbed out of the carriage before they could see her tears. "Come on, Waterloo," she said, throwing an arm over the horse. "We've got to save Papa."

Chapter Twenty-two

On the road into the city, Andrew slowed his winded horse to a walk. It was either do that or risk the animal dying on him. He couldn't kill a faithful mount, no matter how angry he might be at Bridget.

If only the boy had been able to give him more information. But Ned hadn't known much. Only that "the lady," as he called Bridget, had been real upset and told him he had to get his Lordship to come home right off.

Andrew cursed, a long string of maledictions that exhausted all the words he knew but left him feeling just as resentful as ever. Things had been going so well for them. Why didn't Bridget just tell her father that she wouldn't race? Let the old fool be carted off to debtor's prison till he got home to buy him out. The man knew better than to bet. If he were stupid enough to wager after what had happened to him before, he deserved to go to prison.

Andrew pulled out his watch, glancing at it anxiously. Would he get there in time to stop this charade? Bridget ought to have known, or Aunt Sophie at least, that if they paid the man's debts he couldn't be sent to prison. Why hadn't they done just that, paid what Durabian owed? Aunt Sophie was well set up; she could afford it.

Bridget was entirely too good-hearted, letting people take advantage of her. Her letter, obviously written in haste and trepidation, didn't tell him very much. Only that he must hurry home, that she *had* to race or her father's freedom would be forfeit. And that she begged his forgiveness.

Forgiveness! How could he forgive her when she had promised, promised so vehemently, so tearfully, never ever to race again?

He would blister her ears, the foolish chit, for causing him so much trouble. All that haste in leaving Scotland— he hoped in his rush to get away he hadn't ruined things there. And since then he'd been riding posthaste back to London, riding so fast that Ned was left behind.

As he neared Durabian's farm, the road grew crowded. He couldn't have run the filly even if she'd been rested— there were too many riders, too many carriages. Had all London turned out to see his wife make a fool of herself?

He dismounted near the gate, tossing Sable's reins to a stableboy. Then he began to elbow his way through the crowd. He was going to find his wife and put an end to this stupidity.

But the area around the track was packed. People stood shoulder to shoulder, waving their hands about, chattering happily. Blacklegs had set up their stands and were shouting out their odds to prospective clients. Oh yes, London wouldn't soon forget this day.

Where was she? He tried to make his way closer to the track, but the press was too tight. He pushed, even shoved, but all he got for his efforts were hard looks and a few muttered oaths.

The crowd did part for a moment and he had a glimpse of her—Bridget in her leather breeches, her red hair tossing as she swung up on the great stallion's back. "Bridget!" he called out. He thought he saw her turn momentarily in his direction. But her expression was blank. Maybe she didn't see him. Or if she did, she wasn't going to admit it.

She turned again, guiding the great stallion toward the track. Damnation! He'd never get to her now. He'd arrived too late to stop this.

"Andrew! Andrew, over here."

He glanced around. That sounded like Aunt Sophie. Of course, she would be here, egging Bridget on. Whatever had possessed these women? He would have a few words for her, too. Some help she'd been!

There she was. And, by God! she was holding a little girl in each hand.

Grumbling, he made his way toward them.

"Andrew," Aunt Sophie cried happily. "I'm so glad you've come. Did you talk to Bridget yet?"

"No." He glared. "I couldn't get to her."

"Well, never mind. You can talk to her later."

"Never mind!" he thundered. "Later! She broke her promise. She's racing!"

"Now Andrew." Aunt Sophie leaned toward him, her expression conciliatory. "Be sensible. She has to save her father."

"And why?" he demanded irritably. "I paid the old reprobate's gambling debts once. Why did he wager again?"

He noted her expression of shock, but he was too angry to care.

"He didn't," she retorted. "Didn't Bridget explain in her letter?"

"Not really. She said she *had* to race to save her father from being sent to debtor's prison. So I assumed he'd wagered again."

"Well, he didn't," Aunt Sophie said firmly. "It was some regular bills he owed to his tradesmen. Wichersham bought—"

"Wichersham? That bastard?" He might have known.

"Yes," Aunt Sophie said. "Wichersham. He's over there by that oak. And do watch your language in front of the children." She pulled the girls closer. "Wichersham bought them up."

He frowned. "Well, why didn't you pay him off instead?"

"Andrew, really. Give us credit for some sense. We tried." She glared at him indignantly. "He wanted the race. He would not take money." She glanced down at the girls. "He said he would take—take—you know. . . . But Bridget refused."

Anger made him almost incoherent. "Take what? What the hell are you talking about?"

"Andrew! Please! Your language." She looked around and lowered her voice. "Didn't her father tell you what Wichersham said before—before you and Sable raced Waterloo?"

What had that to do with it? "Yes, he told me that Wichersham said he would take the stallion in lieu of the money. That's why Durabian arranged the race."

Aunt Sophie nodded. "And?"

216

"And what?" Andrew asked suspiciously. "I suspect he fixed the race, but I didn't ask him."

"He told you no more? No more than that?"

His temper, never the evenest, threatened to erupt. "Only that he owed Wichersham. Great galloping cannonballs, Aunt Sophie! Will you tell me the whole thing? Now!"

Aunt Sophie slowly turned red. "He—He said he would take the horse—or—or her."

"Her whom?" Andrew demanded. Why must the woman talk in riddles?

Aunt Sophie met his gaze squarely. "Or Bridget. Wichersham told her father before the race that he wanted to set Bridget up in—" She glanced again at the girls and lowered her voice still more. "Set her up in keeping."

A great surge of anger pounded through him, closing his hands into fists. "You're telling me he wanted to—" He stared at her. "I'll kill him! I'll kill the dirty bastard!"

"Andrew, please." Aunt Sophie glanced around them in obvious embarrassment. "Restrain yourself. We don't want all London to know about this. Besides, you cannot *kill* the man. It just isn't done."

"Perhaps not," Andrew said fiercely. "But I can beat him to a pulp. And I will."

And before she could stop him, he set out through the crowd toward the oak where Wichersham was holding court.

As she waited for the starter to give the signal, Bridget leaned forward, caressing the stallion's neck. "Good Waterloo," she crooned. "Let's win this race now."

Waterloo tossed his head as though to say, "Of course

we'll win," and heartsick as she was, Bridget had to smile.

At least Waterloo loved her. He would never desert her. She swallowed over the lump in her throat. Had that been Andrew she'd glimpsed in the crowd—Andrew with a face like a thundercloud?

She tried to tell herself she'd been mistaken. When Andrew got home from Scotland, he would forgive her. But she knew better. That *was* Andrew out there, all right, and he was mad as he could be. And with every reason. She had broken her promise, so she would have to leave him.

The thought tore at her heart, made her eyes fill with tears. She loved Andrew. She loved him so much she didn't know how she would live without him. But she would learn, she told herself as the horses took off and the stallion settled into his stride. She would learn because she had to. Just as she had to ride in this race to save Papa from going to prison.

Impervious to everything but the object of his anger, Andrew made his way through the crowd. He was vaguely aware of startled looks and muttered imprecations from those he jostled aside in his passage, but he paid them no more heed than he did the race itself, now taking place on the track. He'd had enough of Wichersham's nefarious schemes. This was all going to stop. And right now.

The man was standing, his back to the oak, pontificating to the cronies gathered round him. "Of course," he was saying in that raspy irritating voice of his, "Bridget may know horses and—"

When Andrew came to a halt in front of him, Wichersham laughed, the most infuriating, unsettling sound Andrew had heard for a long time.

"Why, if it isn't Haverly!" Wichersham cried. "Come to see his—lady race." He smiled evilly at his sycophants. "As I was saying, Bridget may know horses but—"

His words were cut off in mid-sentence when Andrew grabbed him by the waistcoat and yanked him away from the tree.

"That'll be enough about *my wife*," Andrew commanded, shaking the man roughly to and fro. "If ever I hear her name has passed your lips again, you'll rue the day. And you'll be getting more of *this!*"

In one swift motion he released Wichersham's waistcoat and dealt him a punishing facer, right to the nose. Wichersham went down, hitting the grass with a satisfying thud. He lay there, his bulging eyes wide and staring, his hand pressed to his bloody nose. The coward didn't even offer to get up—or fight back. And his so-called friends faded quickly away.

Andrew snorted in disgust. "I'm telling you. Leave my wife alone. Or next time it'll be pistols." And he stalked off, satisfied with himself, if with nothing else.

He had gone some feet when a great roar went up from the crowd. He whirled in time to see Waterloo cross the finish line—the winner, if that was any help.

Now what should he do? Was he supposed to go to the winner's circle and pretend to be proud of his wife? Proud! When he wanted nothing more than to put the spoiled chit over his knee and give her a good thrashing!

No, he wouldn't go to her. Let her come to him, let her beg forgiveness for this debacle.

When he reached Aunt Sophie, she was practically

jumping up and down, and the little girls with her—their faces all alive with smiles. "She won! Bridget won!" Aunt Sophie cried. The little girls echoed her. "The lady won!"

They were all possessed! And Bridget was the worst of them—the instigator of this madness.

She came slowly through the crowd toward them, her face pale and worried, her white shirt and those godawful breeches streaked with dust and sweat. He stood waiting, his anger almost choking him.

She reached him and stopped, looking hesitantly up. "Andrew," she whispered. "You came."

"I got here too late," he growled, "to stop you from this stupidity."

"My—My letter," she faltered, her face going even paler. "Did you get my letter?"

"Yes. Such as it was." Why must she be so beautiful, even in her distress, that he wanted to clasp her in his arms and forgive her anything?

He hardened his heart. She wouldn't get by him that easily. He wasn't going to forgive her yet.

"I. . . ." she mumbled, hanging her head. Then she straightened her shoulders and looked him square in the eye—her own filling with tears. "I have broken my promise," she said firmly. "And I am sorry. I had good reason—" She swallowed. "Or thought I had. My Papa—before—"

"I know," he said brusquely. "Aunt Sophie told me the whole sorry story."

Hope flickered in her eyes and then went out. "Then you know why I rode. That doesn't excuse it, of course." She looked toward the girls, hanging onto to Aunt Sophie's hands, their little faces solemn. "So I will keep my word. I'll leave your house and take the girls with me. Just as soon as I can get ready."

His breath left him in a great whoosh of air. By God, she actually meant to leave him! In all his anger, he'd never really considered she'd do *that*. And in that instant he saw, with appalling clarity, the rest of his life—a life empty of Bridget, empty of love. And the image was more than he could bear.

"No!" The word shot from his mouth. "You may not take the girls."

Bridget stared at him, not understanding. "Can you care for them yourself? Well, I suppose you can," she went on, answering her own question. "Mrs. Purvey knows what to do and they—"

"Bridget, me girl!" Durabian came grinning through the crowd. "Ye won! Yer the greatest rider ever was!"

"Thank you, Papa." Bridget turned to him. "I—I'll be coming back to live with you." She paused, obviously overcome with emotion.

Durabian turned on him, then, his face reddening. "I collect Bridget told ye about the race what made ye a married man. It weren't her fault. 'Twere all mine. I did it all. To save 'em both—me girl and the stallion. But I didn't think ye'd be holding it against her. What kind a man—"

"It's all right, Papa," Bridget interrupted, clasping his arm. "This isn't about that. This is about me. I promised Andrew not to race, you see, and I broke my promise."

"Promise?" Durabian said, clearly surprised. "I didn't know ye prom—"

"I know, Papa. I didn't tell you because I thought you might not let me ride and—"

"Sure and I wouldn't!" the old man cried. "Not when ye'd promised."

"But I had to, you see, because of what you did for me."

She faced Andrew again. "I knew I might have to leave. I was afraid you wouldn't be able to forgive me."

"Man!" Durabian cried. "How can ye be so cold-hearted? And to yer own wife what loves ye, can't ye see? And—"

"Papa," Bridget said with great dignity. "That's enough. We don't beg."

She'd never looked more beautiful than she did standing there in her leather breeches, her hair all tousled, her face so firm in resolve.

"I knew what I was doing. And I'd do it again." She looked to Andrew, her face white. "I can't leave the girls with you, though I suppose it might be better for—"

"No," he said again, finally finding his voice. "No. You can't take them. You're not going anywhere. You can talk horses all you want. You can ride astride through the streets of London. You can race every day of the week. God knows, you can even take in more children! But you can't leave me, Bridget, you just can't."

He thought that would bring her into his arms, but though she had begun to smile, she held her ground. "Why, Andrew?" she whispered up at him. "Why can't I leave you?"

And oblivious to the crowd around them, he thundered it out: "Because! Because I love you!"

She came into his arms then, raising her face for his kiss. For a moment he was aware of Durabian and Aunt

Sophie congratulating him, the little girls laughing in delight. And then he was aware of nothing but the woman in his arms, the woman he would always love—the woman who was whispering, "Oh Andrew, I love you."

ABOUT THE AUTHOR

NINA PORTER is the pseudonym for Nina Coombs Pykare, who started college at 32, earned her Ph.D. in English at 42, and sold her first book four years later. Since then, she has had forty novels published, including the Zebra Regency romances, LADY FARRINGTON'S FOLLY and THE MATCHMAKER'S MATCH. Nina, who also works as a writing instructor, says she loves dogs, horses, and the West; and she believes that "love is the most important thing in life." She has four sons and a daughter, two grandsons, four granddaughters, and a grandbaby on the way. A resident of Warren, Ohio, Nina says she lives with the hope of finding her own "hero, the most important man in my life."